THE GO AHEAD BOYS AND THE RACING MOTOR-BOAT

ROSS KAY

The Go Ahead Boys and the Racing Motor-Boat

Ross Kay

© 1st World Library, 2010
PO Box 2211
Fairfield, IA 52556
www.1stworldlibrary.com
Second Edition

LCCN: 2009942648

Softcover ISBN: 978-1-4218-5027-6
Hardcover ISBN: 978-1-4218-5125-9

Purchase *"The Go Ahead Boy and the Racing Motor-Boat"*
as a traditional bound book at:
www.1stWorldLibrary.com/purchase.asp?ISBN=978-1-4218-5027-6

1st World Library is a literary, educational organization
dedicated to:

- Creating a free internet library of downloadable ebooks.

- Hosting writing competitions and offering book
publishing scholarships.

Interested in more 1st World Library books?
contact: literacy@1stworldlibrary.com
Check us out at: www.1stworldlibrary.com

1st World Library Literary Society

Giving Back to the World

"If you want to work on the core problem, it's early school literacy."

- James Barksdale, former CEO of Netscape

"No skill is more crucial to the future of a child, or to a democratic and prosperous society, than literacy."

- Los Angeles Times

Literacy... means far more than learning how to read and write... The aim is to transmit... knowledge and promote social participation."

- UNESCO

"Literacy is not a luxury, it is a right and a responsibility. If our world is to meet the challenges of the twenty-first century we must harness the energy and creativity of all our citizens."

- President Bill Clinton

"Parents should be encouraged to read to their children, and teachers should be equipped with all available techniques for teaching literacy, so the varying needs and capacities of individual kids can be taken into account."

- Hugh Mackay

CONTENTS

PREFACE

Every normal boy loves a motor-boat, but words fail to express his enthusiasm when that boat is also a racer. Behind the events recorded in this story are certain facts, so that the tale is largely true. The author will be glad if the account of life in the open, the adventures and fortunes, good or ill, the contests and exciting experiences interest his readers even partly as much as they did the boys who shared in the actual occurrences. I have tried to write a story filled with action, but devoid of sensationalism and false representations. If my boy friends enjoy the company of the Go Ahead boys I shall feel repaid for my labor.

Ross Kay

CHAPTER I

THE START

"Here we go!"

"We're off!"

"Look quick, or we'll be out of your sight."

The long, low motor-boat glided smoothly out from the dock to which it had been made fast. Behind it the water boiled as if it had been stirred by some invisible furnace. The graceful lines of the boat, its manifest power and speed, formed a fitting complement to the bright sunshine and clear air which rested over the waters of the Hudson River.

On the dock, which the Black Growler was leaving so rapidly behind her, were assembled various members of the families represented by the four boys on board the motor-boat. Younger brothers and sisters, two uncles, several aunts, not to mention the various fathers and mothers united in a final word of farewell. Handkerchiefs were waved and the sounds of the last faint call came across the intervening waters.

The Black Growler was leaving Yonkers to be gone more than a month. The trip was one to which the Go

Ahead boys had looked forward with steadily increasing interest.

In the first place the boat belonged to Fred Button, one of the quartet. Fred now was at the wheel and the expression of pride on his face as he occasionally glanced behind him at his companions was one that indicated something of the feeling in his heart. And indeed there was a substantial basis for Fred's pride. Among the many boats on the river the Black Growler moved as if she belonged in a class of her own. People on board the cat boats or yachts, and even the passengers on a great passing steamer, all stood looking with manifest interest at the dark-colored little boat which was speeding over the waters almost like a thing alive.

Fred Button, the owner and present pilot of the swift motor-boat was the smallest, or at least the shortest, of the four boys. His age was the same as that of his companions, all of whom were about seventeen. His round body and rounder face were evidences that in time what Fred lacked in length he might provide in breadth. Among his companions he was a great favorite and frequently was called by one of the several nicknames which his comrades had bestowed upon him. Peewee or Pygmy, the latter sometimes shortened to Pyg, were names to which he answered almost as readily as to his Christian name.

His most intimate friend of the four was John Clemens, whose nickname, "String," indicated what his physique was. He was six feet three inches in height, although his weight was not much more than that of the more diminutive Fred. "The long and the short of it" the two boys sometimes were called when they were seen together.

Grant was the one member of the Go Ahead boys who easily led in whatever he attempted. His standing in school was high and his time in the hundred yards dash stood now as a school record. His fund of general information was so large that some years before, in a joke he had been dubbed Socrates. That expressive name, however, had recently been shortened to Soc.

George Washington Sanders, one of the most popular boys in his school, frequently was referred to as Pop, by which designation his friends indirectly expressed their admiration for one who, even if he bore the name of the Father of his Country, was laughingly referred to as the Papa of the Land. This nickname in the course of time had been shortened to Pop.

Already the four Go Ahead boys had had several stirring experiences in their summer vacations. One of these had been spent at Mackinac Island where their adventures had been chiefly concerned with Smugglers' Island. Together they had made a voyage to the West Indies where their experiences on a desert island have been already recorded.[1] Together they had investigated the mysteries connected with an old house near George's country home, a place shunned by the country folk because of its reputation of being haunted.[2] Another delightful summer had been spent by the boys in a camp in the Canadian woods.[3] All these experiences had only prepared the way for the days which now were confronting them.

[1] See "The Go Ahead Boys and The Treasure Cave."

[2] "The Go Ahead Boys and the Mysterious Old House."

See "The Go Ahead Boys and the Island Camp."

Every one was confident that the Black Growler would give a good account of herself in the motor-boat races which were to be held on the St. Lawrence River. The grandfather of Fred Button, who was the fortunate owner of an island in the majestic river, had invited the boys to spend a month with him in his cottage. Incidentally he had explained that their visit would be at the time when the boat races occurred, which he had no question they all would greatly enjoy. He was unaware that Mr. Button had already purchased a motor-boat of marvelous speed, although at the time he had no thought that it would be entered in any contest or races.

Yielding to Fred's persuasions at last his father had somewhat reluctantly given his consent for the boat to be entered, as well as for Fred to invite the other three Go Ahead boys to spend the coming weeks together on the island.

All these thoughts were more or less in the minds of the Go Ahead boys when the Black Growler swiftly started on her long voyage.

"Are you going to keep her going like this all the time?" demanded John as the swift little boat steadily continued on her way.

"She doesn't like to slow up," replied Fred glancing behind him as he spoke.

"She had better slow up than blow up," retorted John.

"No danger of that," laughed Fred. "The first thing you

know we'll be in the canal."

"I hope not," laughed Grant. "It will be a great day when the Go Ahead boys learn how to use the English language. You don't mean 'in' the canal, you mean 'on' the canal."

"Perhaps he means what my grandfather used to call the 'ragin' canawl'," suggested Grant.

"Maybe we'll be both in it and on it," laughed Fred. "If we should happen to strike a rock or bump into another boat it wouldn't be very hard to understand what would follow."

"That makes me think," said Grant solemnly. "Are you sure that you know how to steer? If we were traveling on the Erie Canal as they used to go soon after it was opened -"

"When was that?" broke in George.

"1825. The Erie Canal extended from Albany to Lake Erie and was constructed chiefly because DeWitt Clinton worked for it with might and main from 1817 to 1825."

"Good for you!" laughed George, "It's pretty hard to trip up old Soc when it comes to figures. Now, I myself happen to know how long the canal is and so I shall be able to tell whether you reeled off your figures, depending upon our ignorance or whether you gave them because you knew what they are. How long is the Erie Canal?" he added slowly.

"Three hundred and fifty and one-half miles, though I

find some authorities give it as three hundred and fifty-two miles," laughed Grant.

"Splendid! Splendid!" retorted George solemnly. "I suppose you know all about all the other great canals too."

"I have looked them up," replied Grant simply. "I don't believe in starting off on a trip like ours without finding out some of the facts connected with it."

"Don't ask me! Don't ask me!" protested John quickly. "I haven't been looking them up, so I don't know."

"I didn't say I was going to ask you," retorted Grant. "I told you I was going to inform you. I looked them up for the benefit of my benighted companions. Now there's the Cape Cod Canal," he added. "I don't believe there's one of you that knows anything about it."

"If we don't stop you, there won't be one of us that doesn't know all about it," said John, pretending to be discouraged by the attitude of his friend. "I suppose we'll have to have it," he added solemnly, "so the sooner we get it out of the way the better. Tell us and have it over with."

"The Cape Cod Canal," said Grant as he looked sternly at John, "is eight miles long, it is twenty-five feet deep and one hundred feet wide."

"My, now I am almost ready to go back home!" said George solemnly. "I cannot imagine finding out anything more important than that. Have you noticed these Palisades we have been passing? Did you ever see anything more beautiful than the river? Pretty soon we'll come to the Highlands and to West Point and I want to say to you right now, Soc, that I would rather know about these things than I would to hear about a ditch that is one hundred feet wide and twenty-five feet deep and eight miles long. What's the good of knowing that anyway?"

"I shall try to improve your mind before we come back home," said Grant, shaking his head.

"You don't expect to accomplish much in just a month, do you?" interposed George.

"Not much more than to get ready to prepare to begin to start to commence on the contract."

"My, what a fluent talker my friend is!" said George. "He never is at a loss for a word. It doesn't make any difference to him whether he knows what it means or not."

"Never mind your old facts and figures," spoke up Fred. "I want you to notice that big! black yacht yonder. Isn't she a beauty?"

"She is that," replied Grant with enthusiasm. "I can almost make out her name," he added as he looked through the field-glasses. "There it is C-a-l-e-Caledonia," he added quickly.

"They have got quite a good many people on board," suggested George as he noticed a group of boys and girls near the rail, who apparently were as deeply interested in the motor-boat as the Go Ahead boys were in the big, black yacht.

"Let's have a race with her," suggested George. "Start her up, Fred, and see if the yacht will try to keep up with us."

Fred laughingly complied with the request, although neither of his companions had any suspicion of the many experiences they were to have with the passengers and crew of the Caledonia before either vessel returned to New York.

CHAPTER II

ON THE WAY

The proposed race, however, did not take place. The graceful Caledonia steadily continued on her way without increasing her speed. There were calls from the deck where the boys noticed several young people standing near the rail. It was plain that there was great admiration on each boat for the beauty and speed of the other. There were calls and cheers, and waving of handkerchiefs to express their feelings. Perhaps it was in part due to this fact that the Black Growler soon began to pull away from the larger boat and not long afterward the Caledonia was left far behind.

"That's the kind of a boat I'm going to have when I get rich!" said George enthusiastically. "I should like to spend about four months a year on board a craft like that."

"That's all right," spoke up Grant, "but I think after about two months of it you would want something else. You see I know you better than you know yourself."

"Yes, I see," retorted George sharply. "You make me think of what Josh Billings said that 'it's a good deal better not to know so many things than it is to know so many things that ain't so!' "

"Never you mind, fellows," spoke up Fred. "This boat suits me all right. You wait until you see that cup the Black Growler is going to win."

"I hope we shan't have to wait too long," said John dryly.

"You'll wait until the race comes off," declared Fred. "I'm not taking any cups before I win them, but when the time comes you wait and see me run away from any boat that tries to keep up with us. I have been on the St. Lawrence before and unless there is something a good deal better than I have ever seen there, we shall simply show our heels to any motor-boats on the river. And they say there are more motor-boats between Clayton and Ogdensburg than anywhere else in America."

"How many?" inquired John.

"I have been told that there are more than a thousand."

"Well," said George, "I'm deeply impressed by the modesty of Peewee. He simply thinks this boat will outclass nine hundred and ninety-nine others that will be madly chasing him all summer long, trying to keep pace with him."

"But he hasn't won the cup yet," said Grant quietly.

"That's right. That's right," spoke up Fred, pretending to be annoyed by the bantering of his friends. "There are always some people that try to take the joy out of life. I heard of an old man the other day who was so disgruntled that when he met a friend on the street who saluted him with a hearty 'good morning' this old man looked all over the sky to make sure he couldn't find a cloud somewhere and say that it wasn't a 'good' morning."

"What did he do if he didn't find any?" laughed George.

"Why he put his hand on his stomach as if he had a pain and shook his head and closed his eyes and groaned out, 'Yes, it's a fine day, but I am sure it is a weather-breeder. We'll have rain to-morrow.'"

"Do you know there are a lot of people like that?" said George. "I met an old woman up near our farm one summer who always said when anybody asked her how she was that she 'enjoyed' poor health. And I guess she did. I never knew any one who took such pride in her aches and pains as she did. One day when the doctor had been to see her she had told him all the pains she suffered and the poor old doctor had to sit there and listen to her for almost an hour. Finally, when he left she started out of the house after him calling to him to come back because she had just thought of another ache that she hadn't told him about."

The boys laughed and silence for a time rested upon the little boat. The Black Growler was moving swiftly and still was attracting attention from every boat she met. Following the channel they kept well out in the river, but the towering hills and the attractive shores were all within sight and manifestly did much to impress the Go Ahead boys.

"Tell me, Fred," spoke up John at last. "Do they have

these races on the St. Lawrence every summer?"

"They have had for the past few years and they have had water sports too."

"What do you mean?"

"Oh, they have swimming, tilting contests, canoe races, diving and I don't know what all."

"Did you ever go in any of them?" inquired John.

A solemn expression came over Fred's face as he said, "Yes, once."

"What did you go into?"

"I tried to walk the greased pole. There was a silver cup on the end of it and the fellow who could walk out and take it could claim it."

"Did you get the cup?"

"I did not," replied Fred shortly.

"I'm surprised, Peewee. I don't know a fellow in all my acquaintance that I think could walk better on a greased pole than you."

"Huh," muttered Fred. "You ought to have seen me. That pole was a part of a telegraph pole. It stuck out from the dock about fifteen feet. It was covered with grease and the grease had been rubbed in."

"How many times were you allowed to try?" asked George.

"Five."

"And you couldn't go in five trials?"

"I didn't go. The first time I stepped on the pole my feet flew out from under me and I sat down on the river about six or seven feet below. I sat down hard too."

"Did you enjoy it?" laughed John.

"I did not," replied Fred slowly, "but the people on the docks and along the banks seemed to have a fine time."

"What did you do next?" laughed George.

"I tied some old sacking on my feet and tried to wipe up the grease as I went along."

"And didn't that work?"

"Nay, verily it didn't work. I took my seat that time on the pole and then when I slipped, I tried to throw my arms around it. But for some good reason I didn't delay very long, before I dropped with a splash into the St. Lawrence."

"I hope they will have those things this summer," spoke up John.

"You would be a good one to walk on a greased pole," said George soberly. "You wouldn't take much space and if you could once get a footing you could reach forward almost to the end and grab the cup."

"If I did," retorted John, "you can rest easy that I

wouldn't let go of it."

"How soon do we come to West Point?" inquired Grant.

"In about an hour," answered Fred.

"Do you know, I sometimes think I should like to go there," said George.

"Couldn't be done, my son," spoke up John.

"Why can't it be done?"

"Because a fellow that enters West Point has to pass an examination."

"Don't you think I could pass it?" demanded George as his friends laughed.

"It depends on what it is," answered John.

"If they would examine you about the old Meeker House and running tin tubes from the kitchen into the front room and a few other things like that maybe you would pass."[4]

[4] See "The Go Ahead Boys and the Mysterious Old House."

"That's all right," spoke up George promptly. "I know something about what a fellow has to do before he passes the West Point examinations anyway and that's more than some fellows I know can say."

"What do you know that we don't?" inquired John.

"How old does a fellow have to be to enter West Point?" demanded George.

"I don't know," replied John somewhat foolishly. "I suppose he has to be about eighteen, at least I suppose a fellow eighteen could enter."

"Could he enter if he was twenty-one?" inquired George.

"He could," spoke up Grant. "A fellow has to be between seventeen and twenty-two years of age before he can take the preliminary examinations. But there's another qualification almost as necessary," he added. "He has got to be free from infirmities."

"No hope for Pop then," said John solemnly. "He has too many infirmities."

"What, for example?" demanded George.

"His appetite is abnormal, his confidence in himself colossal, his willingness to condescend to the level of his superiors is -"

"You're getting all mixed up," interrupted George. "A fellow has to pass a good physical examination and that is all there is to it. Of course if he has too long a tongue or too small a head it might shut him out."

"Of course," assented John. "How does a fellow get a chance to try the examination anyway?"

"He has to be named by his congressman. Most of them, I guess, have a preliminary examination for all the boys that want to enter and then select the one who passes the best examination. But even if he passes, his troubles have only begun, for they make every fellow work his way."

"The government appropriates some money for every cadet, doesn't it?" inquired John.

"Yes," replied George, "$709.50 per year. That is supposed to cover the necessary expenses. It is not only hard work but the boys don't get but one leave of absence in all the course, and even that isn't given until after the first two years."

"But they have vacations, don't they?" inquired John.

"If you want to call them vacations," laughed Grant. "From about the middle of June to the end of August the cadets go into camp. They are busy every day."

"What does a fellow have to pass an examination in in order to enter West Point?"

"English grammar, English composition, algebra through quadratic equations, plane geometry, descriptive geography, physical geography, United States history and the outlines of general history."

"I think I'll go if that's all," laughed John, who was well known to have troubles with most of his examinations in school.

"Look at that boat over yonder!" suddenly interrupted Fred, pointing to a motor-boat about one hundred feet away. "It looks to me as if it was trying to pass us."

"That's just what it is trying to do," said Grant eagerly.

"Don't you let them do it, Peewee."

"That's just what I intend not to do," said Fred resolutely.

In a moment the speed of the Black Growler was increased, but it was also manifest as the boys glanced behind them that the boat they had noticed was in swift pursuit.

CHAPTER III

JOHN DISAPPEARS

The rival boat was distant about one hundred feet, moving in a line nearly parallel with that which the Black Growler was following.

"I believe I have seen that boat before," muttered Fred. "Can any of you fellows make out the name?"

George hastily took the field-glasses and gazed earnestly at the swiftly moving boat. "I can make out some of the letters, Fred," he said slowly. "I can see v-a-r, the next letter looks like n."

"What's that?" demanded Fred abruptly.

"I can't make out the whole of it yet," answered George. "I don't see what Varn spells anyway."

"You better look again," suggested Fred. "I think I know the boat. I guess it's the Varmint."

"That's it," said George quickly. "Only there's something right after the word. I can't just see what that is."

"Here, let me take those glasses," said Grant quickly. "I don't believe you can find anything. Your mother told me that she doesn't want any better evidence that your clothes are hanging in the right places in the closet than for you to say that you had looked for them and they aren't there."

"Listen to the words of our modest friend," said George as he handed the glasses to his comrade. "Grant is a good boy. The only difficulty with him is he doesn't realize how good he is."

"If he doesn't," spoke up John, "it isn't because he doesn't try."

"Keep still, fellows," said Grant, waving his hand at the other Go Ahead boys. "I'm just about to find out what the name of that motor-boat that is beating us -"

"'Beating' us nothing!" interrupted Fred. "Can't you see that she isn't gaining a foot?"

"I can't even see her name yet," said Grant. "You had better slow up a bit, Pygmy. That will give you a good excuse."

In response, Fred increased the power of the fast moving motor-boat.

"I have it. I have it," called Grant exultantly a moment later. "It is Varmint II."

"It is what?" demanded Fred quickly as he glanced behind him for a moment.

"Varmint II, that's what it is," said Grant positively. "What do you know about that?"

Fred was silent a moment before he replied. "Two years ago when I was visiting at my grandfather's I saw the Varmint run away from all the boats in the race. This must be a new one and if she's swifter than the other one then there will be some race, let me tell you. I'm going to try her out a little now."

In accordance with his words Fred changed the course which the Black Growler was following until he was nearer the rival boat. It was plain now that the crew of the Varmint II were deeply interested in the Black Growler. They were watching her movements and eagerly talking to the man at the wheel.

For several minutes the race continued and then abruptly the Varmint II shut off part of her power and speedily dropped behind.

"I told you what would happen," said Fred exultantly. "I would like to run away from that boat in a race. There isn't a boat on the St. Lawrence I would like better to beat."

"But you don't even know she is going to be on the St. Lawrence or in that race," suggested John.

"That's right. That's right," said Fred dolefully. "There's always somebody taking the joy out of life. You mark my words, that boat is going to the St. Lawrence and we'll find her in the race when we leave the stake."

"I hope so," said Grant. "It will be a great race if she's in it! But honestly, Fred, if you knew a little more about steering a boat I think you could win from her. How would it do for you to get somebody to steer, the day of the race?"

"That's right," spoke up George quickly. "All the Black Growler needs is a pilot."

"That - is - most - certainly true," said John slowly, winking at Grant as he spoke.

"Huh," spoke up Fred. "It's a pity there isn't enough gray matter somewhere in this crowd to spell me at the wheel. I have run all the way from New York and I'm tired and yet there isn't a fellow here who is able to steer this boat."

"Beg your pardon," said John. "Ill steer her with great gladness."

"I don't doubt your 'gladness,'" said Fred. "What I'm afraid of is your ability. If it was Grant now steering and we struck a rock he would never own up that that wasn't the very place he was steering for. However, String, take hold here awhile and give me a rest."

"Where are we going to stop for dinner?" inquired George. "This mad race has brought on an attack of hunger with me."

"That's all right," laughed Fred. "I think the only thing you can say is that you are less hungry some times than others. We can stop anywhere you want."

"Then I say we stop at Poughkeepsie," said Grant.

"Poughkeepsie will do for me all right," said John soberly.

A half-hour later the graceful little motor-boat was lying alongside a dock at Poughkeepsie. Two of the boys had remained on board to guard their possessions while two had gone to a restaurant to purchase a luncheon with which they were to return to the boat.

John and George had volunteered their services for the latter purpose and about fifteen minutes after their departure George was seen returning to the dock, his arms well laden with packages of fruit and sandwiches.

"Where's String?" Fred asked as his friend stepped on board and deposited his packages.

"I don't know. I lost him up here."

"Poor John. Lost in Poughkeepsie. I'm afraid we'll have to advertise."

"There's one thing we won't do though," said Grant.

"What's that?" inquired Fred.

"We shan't wait for him to come before we begin operations."

"It does my heart good to hear you speak so truth-fully," said George, as at once he opened the packages and passed the various articles of food which he had obtained.

So busily engaged were the boys that time passed rapidly and a half-hour later George said, "What do you suppose has become of that fellow? I told you that his mother said that he was worse than I am and couldn't find any of his belongings, but I didn't know that he would lose himself."

"Have you ever been in Poughkeepsie?" inquired Grant soberly.

"I have never stopped here."

"Then I have no need for other explanations. I know what has become of John."

"Then you'll be the one to go and get him."

"I guess not," laughed Fred.

"No, if he doesn't show up within fifteen minutes the Black Growler proceeds gracefully on its way and leaves little Johnnie to come after us. Maybe he can work his way by driving mules for a canal boat."

"There isn't any canal here," said Fred.

"Well, we'll leave it to him to settle the way he will come. We shan't wait for him."

"Who's captain of this ship, anyway?" spoke up Fred.

"That's the question that has often puzzled me too," said Grant soberly.

"Well, I am," said Fred.

"You are? Then let me tell you, Captain Peewee, you will have a mutiny on your hands before you know it. This boat is going on to Albany. We have got to get there to-night and if John doesn't care enough about going with us he will have to take the consequences. Do you know I think he may have lost his nerve and gone back home."

"Don't you believe it," said Fred sharply. "John will be here in a few minutes. He never will lose his nerve."

Fifteen minutes however elapsed and still the absent member of the Go Ahead boys did not return.

When fifteen more minutes had passed, Fred, who had insisted that some investigation should be made and a search for John begun, was overruled by his two companions and in spite of the captain's protests, the Black Growler slipped quickly away from the dock and proceeded steadily on her way up the Hudson.

There were no mishaps although twice Fred stopped to secure fresh supplies of gasoline. No trace of the Varmint II had been seen and if she too was headed for the far away St. Lawrence, there was nothing to indicate the fact. And yet Fred became more positive with the passing minutes that among his rivals in the race in which his own swift motor-boat was already entered, would be found the boat whose pursuit he had found it so difficult to shake off.

The boys by the middle of the afternoon were tired. There was no opportunity for exercise and in spite of the beauty of the region through which they were passing there was a certain monotony in their voyage which at last became wearisome.

The sun was sinking low in the western sky when Fred at last said, "I think we'll make Albany in about an hour."

"Do you think we'll find String there?" inquired George.

"I hope so. If it was any other of the Go Ahead boys I would say we would be sure to find him there, but no one knows what Jack will do. The only certain thing about him is his uncertainty. Don't you remember -"

"I'm telling you," interrupted Grant, "that we'll find John waiting for us at the dock. He knows where we're going to land."

"If String is there I'll agree to pay for the dinner to-night," said George. "My own feeling is that he hasn't left Poughkeepsie yet."

It was still light when at last the Black Growler approached the dock where she was to be tied up for the night. The three Go Ahead boys were peering ahead of them with interest, every one looking among the men on the docks for their missing companion.

CHAPTER IV

THE LOST IS FOUND

"He isn't there," exclaimed George gleefully. "I'm safe on my dinner."

"I believe you are right," said Fred in a low voice after he had glanced along the docks several times searching for his missing friend.

"Of course I'm right," said George. "I am always right. That's the reason why your fond parents wanted me to go with you on this trip. Somebody has to go along who understands modern life, so I reluctantly gave up my own convenience and came along to look after these poor benighted Go Ahead boys."

"Keep quiet a minute, George," said Grant, "we all appreciate your kindness. Just now, however, I would rather see String than hear you."

"Not seeing String you must listen to me," laughed George again. "Let me see, I don't buy the dinner, and it seems to me that one or the other of my friends agreed to provide one if I was mistaken about John."

"No such agreement was made," declared Fred sharply.

"Is that so, Grant?" demanded George, turning to the remaining member of the party.

"It certainly is," declared Grant. "You were the only one to make the offer."

"Then I suppose I shall have to put up with it," said George disconsolately. "Now as soon as we get everything ship-shape, we had better go up to the hotel."

"Shall we take our bags or send down for them?" inquired Grant.

"If we don't take them some one else will," said Fred quickly. "We can lock up everything else, but we don't want to leave anything on board that can be taken away."

"Just as you say," said Grant, as taking his bag in his hand he stepped quickly to the dock.

Already a small assembly had gathered and was commenting upon the beauty of the little motor-boat. The pride of Fred had been satisfied so many times throughout the day that he was not unduly moved now by the words which he overheard. In a brief time he and his two companions were walking up State Street and soon secured rooms for the night in their hotel.

An hour later when they entered the dining-room they were amazed to behold their missing friend John seated at a small table at which there were three places besides the one he had taken.

For a moment the three Go Ahead boys stopped and gazed in amazement at him, and then, without a word being spoken, all three silently advanced to the table which he had reserved and apparently without recognizing the presence of their friend at once seated themselves.

"Why don't you say something?" demanded John, a grin appearing on his face as he spoke.

"I'm going to say something in a minute," said George. "I want to read through this program first to find out what I'm to have for my dinner."

"'Program' is a good word," said Grant soberly. "When George has such a chance to get a square meal he always has a regular program mapped out."

"That's all right," retorted George, without glancing up from the menu card.

"Why don't you say something?" demanded John again.

"My friend," said Grant soberly, gazing a moment at John as he spoke, "words are not adequate to express our feeling. How is it with you?"

"I'm fine," said John. "Why don't you ask me where I have been and how I came to Albany?"

"You're in Albany and that is enough to satisfy all the curiosity we have," said Grant.

"It doesn't satisfy me," said John. "When three fellows run away from you and leave you high and dry in a city like Poughkeepsie why all I can say is that -"

"That's enough to say, Johnnie. That will do," interrupted George, waving his right hand at his friend.

"You are simply mistaken," said John, the grin appearing on his face once more. "I want to tell you that whether you want it or not you are going to hear from me and in more ways than one."

"'Threatened people live long,' " spoke up Fred. "At the same time, String, you'll have to own up that we waited for you as long as we thought we could before we started for Albany. I didn't want to be out after dark in the Black Growler."

"I appreciate all your kind feelings," laughed John. "Now I want you to sympathize with me. I had gone to half a dozen different places doing my best to select certain good things for our luncheon. I had a choice assortment too, let me tell you. Why Pop's eyes would have popped out if he had seen what I had obtained, but alas when I came down to the dock I saw the Growler running up the river as if she was trying to get away from me."

"Did you come up by train?" inquired Fred.

"I did not come up by train," retorted John, speaking deliberately.

"How did you come?" asked George, interested now in spite of his effort to appear indifferent.

"Didn't you see the aeroplane?" asked John.

"Aeroplane? No, we didn't see any," said Grant quickly.

"Well, I didn't either," said John, "so that's one way that I didn't come."

"Oh, leave him alone," said George, "he is just bursting with his story. He wants to tell us and we shan't be able to stop him, so let's have our dinner and you may rest easy that before we are done you'll know all of John's story and some beside. To-morrow it will grow big and fast. It's like the pumpkins out in South Dakota. They say that a man has to be on horseback when he plants them."

"How's that?" laughed John.

"Why the vines grow so fast that the only way he can escape is to put his horse into his best paces. Even then they don't always escape."

"What happens if they are overtaken?" asked John.

"Oh, the pumpkin vines grow right around them and cover them up and choke off their wind and do other various stunts."

"Fine! Fine," laughed John, "My story isn't growing like that though let me tell you. This story is true. It's a complete narrative of truthful John. I was about to turn back and make inquiries when I could get an express train for Albany, when what should I see coming up to the dock but the Varmint II. As soon as the people on board saw me they immediately began to urge me to come with them. They had seen the Growler just pulling out and leaving me in my unfortunate plight."

"I guess they suspected what you had in the basket," laughed Fred.

"That may be," acknowledged John. "At all events it saved them buying a good spread, for they took me on board right away and we trailed you all the way up the Hudson. I tell you, Peewee, it's a comfort to ride in a good boat. That Varmint II can travel! Oh, I don't know how many knots an hour!"

"Can she beat the Black Growler?" inquired Fred anxiously.

"Beat her! Beat her!" retorted John. "Why you would think the Black Growler was standing still the Varmint can pull away from her so fast."

"I don't believe that," said Fred, shaking his head.

"Well, you will have to, for they are going to the same place we are. They have entered her in the motor-boat races and as she belongs to the same class that your tub does you will have a fine chance to see her win the cup. That's about the only chance you'll have too, in my opinion." John winked at George and Grant, who immediately in doleful tones expressed their sympathy for Fred.

"It's too bad," declared George, "after a fellow's father has given him a boat such as the Black Growler to find out that it doesn't stand any show in the race. Now if you had found that out before you had bought the boat, Fred, just think how much money, time, labor, trouble, perplexity, sleeplessness, loss of appetite -"

"Never that," broke in Grant, shaking his head. "All the other things, yes, but loss of appetite, never. Just look at him!"

John insisted upon relating his experiences and increased the interest of his friends in spite of their efforts to appear indifferent when he said there were three young people on board the Varmint, who were expecting to spend the summer on an island near Fred's grandfather's and were also confident that the boat race was to be the supreme event of the summer.

In spite of his declaration that he was not anxious, it was plain to his friends that Fred was somewhat cast down by the glowing reports which his companion had brought concerning the swift rival motor-boat.

"To-morrow we'll be on the 'ragin' canawl,'" said Grant. "Now then, I want to know if there is any fellow in this crowd who knows anything about the world's great canals."

"We don't know anything," said Fred. "We heard you talking this morning, but how much of what you said is true nobody knows, not even yourself."

"It's all true," retorted Grant. "As I told you I wasn't willing to start on a trip like this without knowing something about what I was doing."

"When do you start on that new line?" laughed George.

"It doesn't make any difference," said Grant. "Now the Panama Canal, for example belongs to the United States, doesn't it?"

"It does," acknowledged Fred.

"Well, now as a future citizen of this country just tell me between what places that canal extends. If there is one fellow in this crowd who can give me the right answer I will pay for the dinner for all the Go Ahead boys."

"Panama," said John promptly.

"Panama what?" retorted Grant sharply.

"Why the Panama Canal is located at the City of Panama," said John somewhat abashed by the manner of his friend.

"That's good as far as it goes," said Grant, "but I want to know if you know where the other end of the canal is located."

The three boys looked blankly at one another and for an instant no one spoke.

"The canal extends between Colon and the City of Panama," said Grant hastily.

"That's exactly what I was going to say," said George. "You took the words right out of my mouth. You did it so that you wouldn't have to pay for the dinner to-morrow. I guess every one of us knows where the Panama Canal is."

"All right," said Grant. "I'll take your word for it, if you'll tell me how long it is."

Again there was silence among the Go Ahead boys as they glanced foolishly at one another.

"Of course every young American is sure to know such simple facts as that," said Grant condescendingly, "but for my own satisfaction, I am willing to state that it is exactly fifty and one-half miles long."

"How deep is it?" said Fred sharply.

"It is about forty-one feet," answered Grant promptly. "Of course in the lakes it is deeper than that and it is from three hundred to six hundred and forty-nine feet wide. Why, I don't believe," he continued, "that some American boys I happen to know although they passed right through it, could tell me how long the Sault Ste. Marie Canal is. I have a dim suspicion too that they don't know what it connects."

"I know that," said George. "It connects Lake Superior with St. Mary's River and Lake Huron."

"I'm glad you're right once in your life," said Grant. "Now tell me how long that canal is."

"I can't tell a lie, Mr. Schoolmaster," said George, "the Sault Ste. Marie Canal is two miles long."

"All right, I don't have to buy the dinner to-morrow," said Grant.

"There may be some other things you'll have to do though," said John. "You're not done with me yet. No, sir," he added emphatically "that is not all!"

CHAPTER V

THE MISSING BAG

Early the following morning the Go Ahead boys were moving swiftly over the waters of the Erie Canal. Most of the country through which they were passing was new to them, and, rested as they were from the voyage of the preceding day, they were deeply interested in the various scenes through which they were moving.

The speedy Growler still aroused the interest of the people who saw the graceful little boat. The speed at which Fred was driving was not as great as when they had been on the Hudson. The stream was narrower and frequently there were long canal-boats to be passed.

The experiences when they arrived at the locks were alike novel and filled with interest. After they had watched the slowly rising waters and several times had been lifted to a different level the novelty, however, wore off and by the middle of the forenoon the Go Ahead boys were beginning to tease one another.

"There's one thing," said John, "that's as fixed as the sun."

Nobody made any response to his startling suggestion and after he had glanced quizzically at his companions

John continued, "No crowd ever left a fellow at Poughkeepsie and went on without him without having to pay the price. I'm telling you, fellows, that just as sure as the sun shines there's something coming to every one of you, and most of all to Grant."

"Why am I selected for this special favor?" demanded Grant quickly.

"If you don't know there isn't any one who can tell you," retorted John. "All I'm saying is that action and reaction are equal, even if the Panama Canal is fifty and one-half miles long."

"Speaking of canals," said Grant. "I want to know if anybody knows how long the Suez Canal is."

"Speak up, Professor," said George dejectedly. "We have got to hear it, so we might as well have it now as any time. How long is it?"

"It's exactly one hundred miles. Now if there's any Go Ahead boy who can tell what the Suez Canal connects, it will be my turn to pay for the dinner."

There was a silence following Grant's words while the Go Ahead boys looked foolishly at one another. Not one of them was able to answer the simple question.

"The Suez Canal," began Grant, "connects the Mediterranean Sea with the Red Sea."

"How do you know?" demanded Fred. "You have never seen it."

"I don't have to see it to know. I have never seen

London, but I am quite confident there is a city by that name. By the way, fellows, if you'll wait a minute I'll show you something I put in my bag. I saved it for a day just like this."

Rising from his seat Grant hastily sought his bag and in a brief time rejoined his companions.

"What's the matter?" demanded John, as he saw an expression of consternation on the face of his friend.

"Matter!" retorted Grant. "Matter enough. Somebody brought the wrong bag."

"Let me see," said John, rising and examining the bag, which Grant had placed on the seat near him. "That's not mine."

"It surely isn't mine," said George.

"I won't claim it either," added Fred as he glanced behind him.

"Well, it isn't mine," said Grant. "Somebody made a mistake at the hotel this morning and instead of giving me what belonged to me they have sent my bag off in some other direction and given me a bag that belongs to some one else."

"Try your keys," suggested John. "Maybe it isn't as bad as you think."

"The keys don't fit," declared Grant after he had tested them all.

"Maybe there's a catch or a trick of some kind. Look

again, Soc, and see if there isn't some way to find out what there is inside that bag. That's about the only way you can tell whose it is."

"I have been trying," retorted Grant sharply. "It's locked and I haven't any key that will fit it."

"It feels pretty heavy," said John as he lifted the bag in question.

"Yes, it's heavier than mine," acknowledged Grant. "I don't see how that porter could have made any such mistake."

"I don't see any way out of it, Soc, but for you to take your bag back to Albany," said Fred.

"I'm not going back," declared Grant. "I'll send the bag back by express and telegraph the hotel to send my bag in the same way to Utica. If they get busy right away it ought to be there by the time we are."

"No use, my dear friend," said John, shaking his head. "Your bag by this time is on its way to Timbuctoo or San Francisco. Some other fellow has it and if he has and isn't making remarks that sound like echoes of yours, it is only because he hasn't yet found out his mistake."

The perplexity in which Grant found himself was increasing. Many of his necessary articles and much of his clothing that he would require on the trip were contained in the missing bag. He was unable to see the sly wink which John gave Fred when the latter looked questioningly at him.

So insistent was Grant that the Black Growler was stopped at Schenectady to enable him to send a telegram to the hotel at which the Go Ahead boys had stopped the preceding night at Albany.

No one had offered to assist him in his task and the boy alone carried the bag which he believed had been given him in place of his own to the express office. There, in accordance with the word which he had already sent the hotel, he shipped the bag to Albany.

When he returned to the motor-boat so engrossed was he with his own troubles that he failed to discover the grin which appeared on the faces of two of the Go Ahead boys.

"You might have offered to go back to get my bag," suggested Grant sharply when he resumed his seat on board.

"Yes, we might," said Fred. "We might have offered to buy a new one for you and fit it out with all the things you need, but we thought we wouldn't. You need the lesson, Soc. You have been telling all the world how to do it so long that it is time for you to begin to find out some things for yourself."

Grant made no reply and indeed he had little to say until the boat stopped at an attractive village where the boys obtained their luncheon.

When the voyage was resumed, Grant's confidence that his own missing bag would be found when they arrived at Utica in a measure served to restore his good nature and throughout the afternoon he took an active part in the bantering in which the boys engaged.

Occasionally Fred relinquished his task at the wheel and permitted his friends to take turns in steering the boat. The banks of the canal were free from rocks and even if the swift little motor-boat was turned from her course no great amount of damage could follow.

There were other boats they were informed that had preceded them and among them the references to the swift Varmint II were frequent.

On such occasions Fred's passengers at once resumed their task of informing their captain how small his chances of winning the race were becoming. Apparently the Varmint had everything her own way.

Fred did his utmost to appear indifferent to the words of his companions, but in spite of it all it became plain to the other boys that he was seriously disturbed by the comments they made.

There were times when, the course being clear, the speed of the Black Growler was increased almost to her maximum. At such times the farmers in the fields stopped in their labors and stared at the motor-boat, which almost seemed to be shooting through the country.

At other times when they were passing through villages or met a heavily laden canal-boat the Black Growler moved slowly and seemed to share in the need of caution.

It was late in the afternoon when at last the little party arrived at Utica.

"We'll go up to the hotel and have our dinner," said

Grant. "I do not know that I owe the rest of you anything, but I'm going to take pity on you and do what I at first thought I wouldn't. I'm going to give you a dinner."

"That's very kind," said John, winking at Fred as he spoke. "Meanwhile who's going to look after our bags?"

"I'm going to find out first if mine is here to be looked after," said Grant. "Come on with me, Jack, and I'll go to the express offices and see if it is there."

John followed his friend, but their labors were not crowned with success when after an absence of an hour they returned to the place where the Black Growler was awaiting them. Not a word had been received from Albany nor had Grant succeeded in finding any trace of his missing baggage.

"Never mind," he said quickly. "I'll have to make the best of it. I'm not going to spoil all the fun of the trip crying over spilled milk."

Again John winked at Fred, but no words were spoken after the boat and its belongings had been left in charge of a man and theboys together had started for their hotel.

It was still light when they returned to the dock and Fred said, "I wonder how it would do for us to go on a bit farther. There are hotels all along the way and I think it would be good fun to stop at some one of those country taverns."

"We're with you," said George. "We want to get all the

experiences we can on this trip."

"I guess it will be something you will remember," said Grant.

CHAPTER VI

IN THE TAVERN

About half-past eight o 'clock the Go Ahead boys returned to the dock where the Black Growler had been left. A hasty examination convinced them that all their belongings were safe. In accordance with the suggestion which had been made they soon decided to set forth on their voyage. Just how far they would go was left undecided.

"I hear," said Fred, "that we can stop at a village half-way between here and Rome. They say it is all right. If we don't like to sail in the night then we can stop there, but if we want to we can keep on until we get to Rome or Oneida. That's about as far as we'll want to go anyway."

"I think it will be good fun," said John, "to travel through the country by night. Perhaps we'll find some more places like the old Meeker House."[5]

[5] The Go Ahead Boys and the Mysterious Old House.

"I'm afraid," laughed George, "that we'll find our ghosts a little more substantial than they were in that old place."

"I wish we could find my bag," spoke up Grant. "It's strange it didn't come to Utica. I left word with the express office though to send it ahead just as soon as they received it."

"Maybe we'll find the ghost of it," suggested Fred.

Meanwhile they had cast off and the Black Growler was moving noiselessly over the waters of the Erie Canal. They were soon beyond the borders of the attractive city, but after they had passed the first village on their way George said quickly, "Fellows, I believe it's going to rain. Look at those clouds over yonder." As he spoke George pointed to some heavy clouds that could be seen massing in the western sky.

"I don't want to get caught out here in a thunder storm," said John.

"We shan't be," said Fred. "I'll put on a little more speed and we'll go on to the next place. That's where the hotel or tavern is that they told me about in Utica. It won't rain before we get there for it is only four or five miles ahead. If it is going to rain we can stop. If it doesn't we can keep on if we want to."

Conversation ceased as the speed of the swift little boat increased. Less than a half-hour had elapsed when the boys found that they were entering the village to which Fred had referred.

"How about it, Fred?" called John. "It looks pretty black to me."

"It does to me, too," replied Fred. "I think the best thing for us to do will be to stop. We'll find a place where we can leave the motor-boat and then we'll go up to the hotel and if we have to we'll stay there all night."

The boys all agreed to the suggestion and in a brief time the graceful little boat was covered in such a way that she was protected from the coming storm, which now was almost upon them.

Hastily the boys took their bags and at once started for the hotel which they were informed was only a few yards distant.

With difficulty they made their way along the darkened street, and in a few minutes arrived at their destination.

Just as they entered, the storm broke. There was a long roll of thunder followed by a blinding flash and then the rain began to fall in torrents.

"Just in time, weren't we?" said Fred with a laugh. "You're always right if you do what I tell you to. It was my suggestion and I am glad that for once in your lives you had wisdom enough to do what I said."

"That remains to be seen," said Grant dryly as he looked about the room in which they found themselves. "It seems to me that the motto over the door of this place ought to be, 'He who enters here leaves soap behind.' "

"Where did you find that?" laughed George.

"Didn't you ever hear of the motto over the Bridge of Sighs?"

Whether the boys had ever heard of the famous bridge or not was not manifest, for at that moment in the midst of a deafening peal of thunder the landlady entered the room where the boys were waiting.

"What can I do for you?" she inquired as the thunder ceased.

"We're caught in the storm and thought perhaps we might stay here all night," suggested Fred.

"The house is pretty full," said the woman dubiously. "I don't know whether I can give you rooms or not."

At that moment there came a burst of loud laughter from the bar-room. It was plain that many of the men who were employed on the canal also had sought shelter in the little tavern. The house was old, so old that the boards in the floor were warped and the low ceilings gave evidence of the many years that had passed since they had been placed there. Not a door fitted its frame and the windows were all small, the panes being not much more than seven by nine. Whatever was done in one part of the house plainly was likely to be known also in other parts. The noisy men, who were drinking in the bar-room, whose shouts and songs and cries now were even more distinctly heard, could not confine their loud demonstrations to the room in which they had assembled even if they had been so inclined.

"If you don't mind," suggested Fred to the landlady, "I think we would like to go up to our rooms."

"Have you had any supper?" inquired the woman.

"Yes, we got some in Utica," replied Fred.

"Where are you goin'?"

"We expect to go to the St. Lawrence River."

"You don't tell me," exclaimed the woman. "How be you goin'?"

"We have got a motor-boat."

"Land sakes! You don't say so! That's a terrible long ways and I don't see how you can get there with a boat all the way."

"The storm caught us and we thought we had better stop here for the night than try to go on any farther."

"Where do you come from?" inquired the woman, who busied herself lighting two candles while she was talking.

"We came from Albany this morning," replied Fred, who did not think it necessary to go more into details concerning their expedition.

"My, you must have come pretty fast. Now, if you'll follow me I'll show you to your rooms."

Fred glanced uneasily behind him as from the bar-room at that moment there came another noisy outburst that was almost alarming in its character.

"How many men are there in there?" inquired Fred, nodding his head toward the room as he spoke.

"It's about full," replied the landlady. "A stormy night like this drives a good many of the boatmen and the hands under cover."

"They are a noisy lot," suggested Fred.

"They are a tough crowd," said the woman feelingly. "Sometimes they go off and don't pay me a cent. That's one reason why I make everybody pay before I give them a room."

"Do you mean that we'll have to pay before we take the room?" inquired John.

"Yes, sir, that's just what I say. That's the rule o' this house."

"Well, I guess we'll see the rooms first then," said George.

Conversation ceased as the woman, who was stout and consequently slow in her movements, led the way up the creaking stairway and then through the hall on the second floor. The floor here also was loose and every step was announced by creakings, while various other sounds were emitted as the boards resumed their accustomed places.

"Here you be," said the woman at last as she stopped before the rooms at the end of the hall-way.

"We're directly over the bar-room, aren't we?" inquired John as another noisy outburst came from below.

"Yes, but you won't mind that after a bit," explained the landlady. "You'll get used to it same as I have. I go to sleep and don't pay no more attention to the noises than I do to the wind that blows."

By this time she had opened the doors, which were unlocked, and entered the rooms.

The boys looked ruefully at one another when they became aware in the dim light of the condition of the rooms to which they had been shown.

"I don't believe those windows have seen soap and water since the Erie Canal was built," whispered George to Grant. "When did you say that was?"

"Keep quiet a minute, Pop," retorted Grant.

The rain was beating against the windows with renewed force. The storm apparently was at its height. For them to go on in the Black Growler was almost impossible. There was nothing to be done, except to make the best of the conditions in which they now found themselves.

Soon after the withdrawal of their landlady, who had been paid in advance for the use of the rooms, although breakfast was not included as the boys explained they might have to leave the village before sunrise, they prepared for bed. They were thoroughly tired by the new experiences of the past day and in spite of their surroundings and the noise of the men below and of the storm, which still was raging, they decided to retire.

Their rooms did not connect and as George and Grant withdrew, Fred said, "If we need your help in the night, fellows, don't fail to come right away."

"Are you scared, Peewee?" laughed George.

"Yes, I am, and I don't mind saying so," retorted Fred. "I don't like the sound that comes from that room downstairs."

Fred's feelings were not relieved when he found it was impossible to lock the doors. An old fashioned iron latch was the only means by which each door was opened and there were not even bolts or buttons by which the door could be fastened.

"I'm going to put a chair against the door," said Fred. "I'm afraid something will happen before morning."

Nor was Fred disappointed, for two hours after the boys were in bed the door of the room which Fred and John occupied was stealthily opened by some one in the hall.

CHAPTER VII

AN UNWELCOME PARTY

"Who's there? Who's there?" demanded Fred sharply.

The noise in the room below had prevented him from sleeping soundly. Several times he sat erect in bed, convinced that some one was in the room. Even when his fears proved to be groundless he was unable to ignore the shouts and songs and calls that frequently indicated that the men in the room below were angry. Before he had retired he had obtained a glimpse of the shouting assembly when a door had been opened and the sight had not soothed his feelings. And now he was positive some one was trying to open the door of their room.

Aroused by the call of his friend, John also quickly sat up and stared about him. There was no mistaking the fact that some one was trying to enter by the door which yielded slightly to the pressure and the chair which had been placed by Fred to protect them had been moved back a few inches from its place.

"Who's there? Who's there?" demanded Fred sharply.

No reply was given to his question although the door slowly was closed again and the sound of the footsteps of some one moving down the hall was plainly heard.

"What do you suppose that was?" demanded Fred in a whisper.

"Somebody was trying to break in," replied John.

"What do you suppose he wanted?"

"He wanted to get in."

"What for?"

"I don't know. You'll have to ask him, I guess," replied John drowsily for by this time he had resumed his place on the pillow.

"I think he wanted our money," suggested Fred.

"He didn't want much then. Maybe he wanted our money and our lives."

"All the same I'm scared. I don't like this place. I don't know why we stopped here. It must be past one o'clock now and yet hear those men yell down there in the bar-room. I'm going to see what time it is."

Fred climbed out of bed and striking a match looked at his watch. "It's quarter past one," he said, but the sound which came from John did not indicate that he was specially interested in the report of the watch.

Fred looked out of the window and saw that the storm long since had passed. The air was cool and fresh and had it not been for the uproar in the hotel the night would have been an ideal one.

Before he rejoined his companion Fred replaced the chair so that it barred the opening of the door.

Convinced that he had done all in his power he climbed back into bed once more and in spite of his declaration when daylight came that he had not been asleep John was not convinced.

"Come on, String," said Fred when once more he had looked at his watch to discover the time. "It's five o'clock. It's time for us to be moving. I wouldn't have breakfast in this hole if they paid me for it."

"Why can't you leave a fellow alone and let him sleep? I'm tired. I got left at Poughkeepsie and I had a hard day yesterday too."

"No, sir," said Fred firmly. "This party starts from this place in thirty minutes. Any one who isn't ready will have to come by canal-boat. The Black Growler leaves here at five-thirty sharp."

With a groan John arose and began to dress, although he protested feelingly all the time against the unreasonable demands of Fred.

The other two Go Ahead boys were speedily aroused and twenty minutes later they departed from the hotel.

"It looks worse in the morning than it does at night and we thought that wasn't possible when we came here last evening," said George when the Go Ahead boys looked behind them after their departure.

"I think I will send that landlady a Christmas present of a cake of soap," said Grant soberly.

"She wouldn't know what it was for," laughed John, "if you did."

"My, I would like to hear what my mother would say if she could see the inside of that old tavern."

"The worst thing of all," said Fred, "was the riot in the bar-room. I didn't sleep a wink last night."

"You didn't sound that way, Freddie," said George.

"What time did the noise downstairs stop, Peewee?" inquired John.

"It didn't stop, I guess," laughed Fred. "The landlady said the storm drove all the canal-men into the house, but it didn't seem to me there was anything that drove them out. I shouldn't like to meet one of those men in a dark alley."

"You don't have to meet them," suggested George. "We have lived through the night somehow and are all safe. Now if the Black Growler is ready we are. We'll get our breakfast at Rome, I suppose."

"That's what we will," said Fred, quickening his pace as he spoke.

"Look yonder!" exclaimed John, abruptly halting as he spoke and pointing in surprise at their motor-boat, which was only a few yards distant.

In response to his suggestion the Go Ahead boys all stopped and stared in amazement at the sight before them.

On board the Black Growler were at least a half-dozen men and it required no explanation to enable the boys to understand that they were a part of the noisy assembly which had made night hideous in the hotel.

"Here," called Fred, running ahead of his companions. "What are you doing in that boat?"

"Who are you?" demanded one of the occupants, turning and facing Fred as he spoke.

"That's my boat," declared Fred.

"You don't say so!" replied the man in shrill tones, at which his companions laughed loudly.

For a moment Fred stopped and stared blankly at the men, who had apparently made themselves fully at home on board his motor-boat. The awnings had been taken in and the self-invited guests had been examining various parts of the fleet little craft.

"Did you ever hear," continued the spokesman, "that possession is nine points of the law and that the tenth isn't worth fighting about? Maybe we'll ask you to prove that this boat is yours. According to the records of my private secretary this here yacht is mine. I'm goin' on a cruise up to Buffalo and I have invited a few o' my pals to come along with me."

The men were a brutal and powerful lot. Every one showed the effect of the night which he had spent in the bar-room. The boys were powerless to compel them to leave the boat if they did not choose to do so.

The predicament in which the Go Ahead boys now

found themselves seemed to appeal strongly to the men on board. They laughed loudly and the leader who had spoken before, said, "Why don't you come on board? If this boat is yours all you have to do is to come and take it."

"It is, all right. That is our boat," said Fred.

"If you don't get out I shall have to get some one to put you out."

"Don't be so unkind, mister," retorted the leader, while his companions again united in a shout of glee. "There aren't many men around this place that will want to undertake that job. If you would really like to have us go ashore it seems to me the best plan would be for you to come and throw us out."

Once more the unwelcome guests laughed loudly at the words of their leader, while the confusion among the Go Ahead boys became more marked.

Withdrawing a few feet from the bank Fred called his companions about him and in low tones they discussed the course of action which they ought to follow.

"We had better go up and get the constable," suggested John. "Get out a warrant for these men. They won't make any trouble even if the constable comes down alone."

"I'm not so sure," said Fred. "What do you think, Grant?"

"I don't believe the men intend to stay on board," replied Grant. "They probably were attracted by the appearance of the Black Growler and when they saw us coming they put up a bold front and just tried to scare Fred."

"What do you think is the best thing to do?" inquired Fred.

"My suggestion is to go back to the boat, not have much to say to the men and get ready to start. They won't bother us, at least I don't believe they will."

"What shall we do if they make trouble?"

"It will be time enough to decide that when we have to," replied Grant. "I'm sure they won't make any trouble after they see that we are going to start."

"All right, we'll try it," said Fred dubiously, and once more returning to the place where the Black Growler was awaiting them, the three bags which contained the belongings of the boys were placed on board and ignoring the bantering of the men, they at once prepared to cast off.

"You don't mean to say we're going to start now, do you?" inquired the leader.

"Yes," said Fred shortly.

"Why, we didn't think you'd go for an hour yet. We haven't got our trunks."

Again his companions laughed loudly at the wit of their leader, but as yet not one of them had made any move to leave the boat.

Fred's alarm was plain in spite of the boldness with which he cast off the bow line. Grant already had performed a similar service with the stern line and the boys were now ready to depart.

"It's nice of you to invite us to go along with you," said the leader. "This is a purty little boat and me and my pals will enjoy a ride in her."

"We're going to start now," said Fred quietly, striving to conceal his fear.

"Why, I guess we're ready, aren't we?" said the leader as he glanced at his companions.

"I reckon we are, cap'n," replied one of the men.

The six men occupied most of the available space on board the little boat. Striving to appear indifferent to their presence Fred advanced to the wheel, turned on the power and prepared to depart.

CHAPTER VIII

THE COMING OF THE CALEDONIA

In response to Fred's action there was a loud shout of protest from the men on board. Every one still was manifesting the effect of the drunken spree through which they had passed the preceding night. As yet, however, they had not offered any violence and although Fred's heart was beating rapidly he resolutely stuck to his task and in a brief time the Black Growler darted forward like a thing alive.

For a moment the uninvited passengers apparently were startled by the unexpected action of the young captain. They speedily recovered, however, from their surprise, and one of the men turning to the leader said, "My, ain 't she purty, Jim!"

"She is that," replied Jim promptly. "She looks better than she did when I took my last trip to Niag'ra. When I left my house on Fifth Avenoo I didn't think she'd ever measure up to what she was that time, but she is goin' one better. Yes, sir, she's all that you say she is."

Still the men did not interfere with Fred in his management of the motor-boat. Apparently too they did not have any objection to the voyage. Indeed the Go Ahead boys already were aware of the fact that every one of their self-invited guests had brought a small bundle with him. They naturally inferred that these bundles contained most of the earthly possessions of their noisy passengers.

"How is it, Jim!" called another of the men. "Isn't it about time we had breakfast?"

"That's right," spoke up another. "I'm hungry, too. Seems to me I would like one o' them grape fruits."

"Grape fruits? You don't know what they be," retorted Jim.

"You tell us what they be," responded the man, unabashed by the rebuke of the leader.

"Don't you know?" retorted Jim scornfully. "Why grape fruit's the stuff that grows on grape vines."

"Get out!" said the other one. "I guess I know enough about the country to know that grapes grow on grape vines."

"In course they do," acknowledged Jim, "but this isn't grapes, this is grape fruit. It takes a special vine to grow it."

"Does it grow right on the vine?"

"In course it does. What do you think, it grows under the ground like tomatoes?"

"Tomatoes don't grow under the ground," spoke up another of the party. "It's potatoes that grow under the ground."

"It's all one," retorted Jim glibly. "Potatoes and tomatoes. I knew one grew in the air and the other grew in the ground."

"What about the grape fruits, Jim?" demanded the first speaker.

"Well, they grow on the vines. They are just like big yeller grapes. Many 's a time out on my country estate I have climbed the ladder and picked 'em from the vines that grow so high they hid the sight of the street from the piazzy of my bungaloo."

"I'm wondering where you got this yacht, Jim," inquired another.

"Never mind how I got it as long as we have got it. That's the main thing," interrupted another one. "What I want to know, is about those grape fruits we're talking about. How does it taste?"

"Fine. Fine," answered Jim promptly. Then turning to the boys he inquired, "Have you got anything on board to eat?"

"You see that monemint up yonder," interrupted another pointing to a tall granite shaft that could be seen in the distance. The entire party including the boys at once looked in the direction indicated and saw a beautiful memorial stone, although few of them were aware of what it commemorated.

"Yes, that's my granddad's tombstone," said one of the tramps.

"I guess he must have been some man," exclaimed one

of his companions. "It's a pity the rest of the family didn't take after him."

"We did, but we didn't want to hog the whole thing. We had to let some one else have a chance too."

Meanwhile the Black Growler was speeding swiftly over the waters of the Erie Canal. Fred was driving at high speed and as the boat sped forward he was keenly watching for the coming of a boat that might provide help for the Go Ahead boys in their predicament.

Several canal-boats had been passed, but there was no one on board who appeared to be able to help.

The unwelcome guests still talked noisily to one another, but in the main they ignored the boys and as yet had not offered any violence.

"Who's running this 'ere boat, Jim?" suddenly spoke up one of the passengers. "I thought you said this was your yacht."

"I did say so," answered Jim promptly. "I'm just taking out a pleasure party. Didn't you never go to no picnic afore? I want you to be good, for we have got comp'ny on board. When you have got guests you have to be perlite whether you want to be or not."

Still the Black Growler was moving swiftly. The waters over which she was passing seethed and boiled as if they had been heated by unseen fires. Even Fred had lost a part of his alarm as he began to suspect that his uninvited passengers did not know how to manage the boat. If they did, it was difficult to understand why they had not yet driven the boys away and taken charge.

There was another thought in Fred's mind that was perplexing. He suspected that the supply of gasoline was running low. He had neglected to have the tank filled the preceding night, believing that he had a supply ample to carry them forward until they could obtain more. Suppose the motor-boat should stop? What would the men do? They might accuse him of deliberately stopping and in that event he was aware that there might be serious trouble. Indeed, he was still puzzled to understand why the men appeared to be so contented. If they had been workers on the canal, or had been employed by any of the boats why was it that they were free this morning? He was aware that the little city of Rome could not be far away.

If once he should be able to bring the Black Growler safely within the borders of the city he was confident he would be able to rid himself speedily of the men, whose presence with every passing moment was becoming more difficult to bear.

He looked eagerly ahead for signs of the city. He was unable to discover any, however, but his fears increased as he became more positive that his supply of gasoline was low. If only it would last a half-hour longer!

On either side of the canal was a level stretch of country and near to the water no houses were to be seen. His friends had taken seats on the deck forward. In low tones they conversed among themselves, but Fred was too busy in his own task either to heed what they were saying or to join in their conversation.

A few minutes later, after the speed of the boat had materially decreased, Fred said abruptly, "We have got to stop."

"What for?" demanded the leader, quickly rising as he spoke and turning toward the young pilot.

"Our gasoline is gone."

"Look here, young fellow," said the leader of the gang after he had silently glared at Fred a moment, "I don't want you to try any of your games on us. We're bad men. Now then, you keep this boat goin'," he added threateningly.

"I only wish I could do it," said Fred.

"Are you givin' us straight goods when you say your gasoline is gone?"

"I am."

"What are you goin' to do?"

"Nothing. That's the trouble. You can't do anything without gasoline. I am thinking of letting some of my passengers go ahead and get enough to carry us into the town. Do you know how far it is to Rome?"

"Must be about three mile."

"That wouldn't be very much of a walk," said Fred glibly.

For some unexplained reason his courage now had returned and he stood in less fear of his rough and noisy guests.

"What are you goin' to do?" again demanded the leader.

"There isn't anything I can do," retorted Fred sharply, "unless some of you will go ahead and get some gasoline."

"That's right, Jim," spoke up one of his companions. "We'll go and get his gasoline. Tell him to give us four dollars and we'll get a good supply."

"That's right," spoke up Jim quickly. "We can't get gasoline without some money."

"Oh, one of us will go along and pay the bills," spoke up John, who up to this point had taken no part in the conversation.

"How much money you got?"

"I guess we have got just enough to buy fifteen gallons of gasoline."

"All right, then, give it to us and we'll get the gasoline for you."

"I told you that we shan't give you the money," said John. "We'll go with you. Perhaps we can get a ride on a canal-boat or something."

"You won't save much time that way," retorted Jim. "The only thing to do is to let us have the money and save yourselves a lot of trouble."

"We're not going to give you any money," said John quietly. "I told you that before. The thing for you to do is to clear out, every one of you if you don't want to help."

Unknown to his companions John had been keeping a careful outlook on the canal behind them. In the distance he had seen a yacht approaching that he was confident was the Caledonia, which they had passed when first they had set forth on their voyage. He was confident also that the coming of the yacht, together with the number of men that comprised her crew, would be sufficient to overawe the half-dozen men that had forced their company upon the Go Ahead boys.

"Yonder comes the Caledonia!" he exclaimed suddenly. "They will give us a lift as soon as they catch up with us."

Instantly the eyes of every one on board the Black Growler were turned toward the approaching yacht.

Apparently the sight had markedly different effects. The Go Ahead boys were elated, but their passengers after a hasty glance and a few words spoken in low tones to one another, instantly seizing their bundles leaped ashore and ran swiftly toward the road which was not more than fifty yards distant.

CHAPTER IX

A FRIEND IN NEED

In response to the signal of distress which Fred waved from the deck of the Black Growler as the Caledonia approached, the speed of the big yacht was checked and she stopped not far from the motor-boat. It was still early in the morning and the owners or guests on board the Caledonia were not seen on deck.

"What's wrong? What's the trouble?" called the captain, leaning over the rail and speaking to Fred.

"We have had trouble," replied Fred. "A gang of tramps or canal men forced themselves on board and we have just gotten rid of them. When they saw the Caledonia coming they all ran."

"Well, if you have got rid of them," said the captain gruffly, "what more do you want? If you go ahead they won't catch up with you."

"But we can't go ahead."

"Why not?"

"Our gasoline is out."

"We don't run by gasoline," said the captain, "and I'm afraid steam wouldn't do you any good."

"Perhaps you might give us a tow as far as Rome."

"Perhaps we might and then -"

"What's the trouble?" Fred looked up quickly as he saw a man about fifty years of age approaching the rail and standing near the captain of the yacht. He wore a yachting cap and it was plain to the perplexed boy that he either was the owner of the beautiful boat or one whose word counted for much.

"We have had our troubles," explained Fred once more. "A gang of tramps forced their way on board our boat and they have just left us. Our gasoline is out and I was asking the captain if he would be willing to give us a tow as far as Rome."

"Of course he will," said the man heartily. "Have you got a painter long enough?"

"I'm afraid not," replied Fred.

"Then we'll toss you a rope."

The captain at once responded to the word of the man who had been speaking to Fred and in a brief time a rope was thrown on board the little motor-boat.

"Are you all ready?" called the man from the deck.

"Yes, sir," replied Fred heartily, for by this time he and his friends had made the rope fast and were prepared to start.

"All right then, captain, go ahead."

The Caledonia at once resumed her way and the Black Growler obediently followed about twenty-five feet behind the larger boat.

Before they arrived at Rome other people, in addition to the man who assisted the boys, were seen on the deck of the Caledonia. It was evident that the party had not followed the example of the Go Ahead boys in spending any nights at hotels. They slept on board and the port-holes of what undoubtedly were beautiful little cabins were plainly seen along the sides of the yacht.

It was manifest too that the story of the misfortunes of the Go Ahead boys was speedily told, for a party of five young people in addition to the older ones assembled in the stern of the Caledonia and laughingly greeted the boys in the boat that was being towed.

A short time afterward the boats entered the little city of Rome. When they arrived at a place where a landing safely could be made Fred shouted to the people on the Caledonia, "We'll cast off now. Thank you for all you have done. You have helped us out of a bad fix."

"You're very welcome, I'm sure," replied the man who had arranged for their relief from their predicament.

"Are you going down the St. Lawrence?" he added.

"Yes, sir," replied Fred, "as far as Alexandria Bay."

"Then we may see you again," called the man. "We expect to be on an island near there. My name is Stevens. If you expect to be in Alexandria Bay very long don't fail to look us up."

"Thank you, sir," replied Fred, and his companions were as interested as he in his word. "We certainly shall do so. Thank you again for all that you have done to help us."

The Caledonia quickly resumed her voyage, while the boys waving their handkerchiefs in response to the tokens of good will that came from the strangers who had helped them, speedily made their boat fast and went ashore.

In response to their inquiries they were directed to a place where they could obtain a breakfast and not many minutes had elapsed before the four Go Ahead boys were seated about a table busily engaged in their repast.

"I tell you I'm hungry," said John as he called for a second piece of beefsteak.

"That's the way you would be all the time," said George, "if you would only get up early in the morning."

"That doesn't go. I was up all night long," spoke up Fred. "I didn't sleep any last night."

"I noticed that," said Grant. "The sound that came from your room showed very plainly that you were not sleeping and yet I cannot understand why a fellow should make all those noises if he is wide awake."

"It was John you heard," retorted Fred.

"Yes, I heard John too," said Grant. "It was a duet most of the time. Now aren't you glad," he added, "that I told you how wide the Erie Canal is? You see there was plenty of room for the Caledonia to pass us and take us in tow."

"How wide is the Erie Canal?" spoke up George. "I don't believe you can remember it now yourself. You haven't your notes with you. None of that," he added quickly as Grant felt in his pocket for a paper. "Tell me on your word of honor how wide the Erie Canal is."

"Seventy feet wide on the surface and fifty-six feet wide at the bottom," said Grant promptly.

"I suppose we'll have to take your word for it," said George as his friends laughed at his discomfiture. "We can't dispute you and even if you don't know anything about it you tell it as if you believed it to be the most solemn truth in the world."

"It's true, just as I'm telling you," said Grant.

"How about the new canal that New York State is building now?"

"I have told you about that too," said Grant, "but then you have to have a good many review lessons with some people."

"That's all right, but just the same tell me about the new canal. How wide is it?"

"That's one hundred and twenty-three to one hundred and seventy-one feet wide on the surface, and seventy-five feet wide at the bottom. Of course there are some places," Grant added, "when it runs into a lake or a pond where it is a good deal wider than that. But as far as the digging is concerned that's the width."

"Is it deeper than the Erie Canal?"

"Yes, sir. The Erie Canal is about seven feet deep and the new one is about twelve feet deep. It's going to be deep enough to take in boats of three thousand tons."

As soon as their breakfast had been eaten, and a fresh supply of gasoline had been obtained, once more in high spirits the boys started in their swift motor-boat.

Their experience with the canal-men now was only a memory and they could well afford to laugh at what had been said and done.

"That's what you get for having us stop in a place such as you picked out, Peewee," said George. "There's no accounting for the tastes of some people. Now, I never should have selected that place."

"You can believe me, I'll never select it again," answered Fred, so soberly that his friends all laughed. "Once is enough and forever. I didn't believe there could be such a place in the whole of New York State."

"Well, you know now there is," said John, "and so do the rest of us. We don't stop again without knowing something of the hotel in which we are to stay."

"Where shall we stay to-night, fellows?" inquired Fred. "We ought to get to Syracuse early this afternoon and we can go right on to Oswego if you want to or we can stay there until to-morrow morning and start then."

"Wait and see what time it is when we strike Syracuse," said Grant. "Probably the gasoline you bought back there at Rome won't last until we get there."

"I have got enough gasoline to take us to the St. Lawrence River," declared Fred. "I'm not going to be caught again as I was this morning."

Meanwhile the Black Growler was noisily speeding on her way. To three of the boys the country through which they were moving was all new and therefore abounded in interest. Prosperous villages and fertile farms were passed. As the sun climbed higher into the heavens the day became so much warmer that the boys were glad to seek the shelter behind the awnings which they now had made use of, as a protection from the heat and glare.

It was early in the afternoon when the Go Ahead boys arrived at the thriving city of Syracuse. They speedily decided to rest an hour after they had stopped for luncheon and then through the Oswego Canal to go on to the shore of Lake Ontario. There they would be ready to start on the following morning and were hopeful that if no mishaps occurred they would arrive at their destination the following afternoon. The clear air, the quiet that rested over the region through which they were passing, the tranquil attitude of even the cattle in the fields gave slight indication that the peacefulness of the scene was soon to be broken and the Go Ahead boys were to enter upon one of their most stirring experiences.

CHAPTER X

IN TROUBLE

The Black Growler was not moving as swiftly as when she had been speeding over the waters of the Erie Canal. There was less need of haste now and the boys were more interested as they were drawing near the city which was to be the destination of their inland voyage.

It was dusk when they arrived at Oswego. They made the little motor-boat safe until the following morning and then with their belongings at once walked to the hotel where they were to pass the night.

A hearty dinner soon revived the spirits of the boys, who were now somewhat wearied by their long voyage from New York.

They visited several places of interest in the little city but at an early hour returned to the hotel and sought their rooms.

The following morning found them soon after an early breakfast once more on board the Black Growler.

They now were about to pass out upon the waters of Lake Ontario. Whatever perils they had experienced from the canal-men were no longer to be faced. If there was danger ahead it would come from the squalls which frequently occurred on Lake Ontario. They were all confident, however, that they would complete the remainder of their voyage successfully and in high spirits prepared to cast off.

"Hi, Peewee!" called George. "Are you sure you have got all the gasoline we need?"

"Yes, sir, I'm sure," laughed Fred. "That's one predicament I'm never going to get caught in again. We may have something else go wrong but we'll not run short of gasoline."

"I'm glad to hear it," said Grant soberly. "I noticed from the sounds that came from your room last night that you weren't sleeping very well again. I didn't know but you would be so tired this morning that you would forget all about the Black Growler and even the Go Ahead boys."

"That's all right," laughed Fred. "Do I look sleepy this morning?"

"Not especially."

"Well, I'm not, whether I look so or not," retorted Fred. "If you are all ready we'll start."

"We're all ready," answered the Go Ahead boys together and a moment later the Black Growler was speeding on her way toward the waters of the open lake.

"My, what a glorious day this is," exclaimed John

when a little later the motor-boat was fast leaving Oswego behind.

Indeed there was much to cause the young sailors to be enthusiastic over the morning. The clear air, the morning sunlight, the sparkling waters of the beautiful lake all combined to produce an effect that was unlike any which the boys before had experienced. Even the waves appeared to be peaceful. Not a whitecap was in sight.

"Did you hear what that man on the dock said when we passed?" inquired Grant.

"What man?" inquired Fred. "What did he say?"

"Why he said we had better take a man along with us that knows the lake."

"No, I didn't hear him," said Fred. "And if I had, it wouldn't have made any difference. I know my way all right and you fellows needn't be afraid that you won't be down among the Thousand Islands in time for dinner."

"Where shall we get our luncheon, Fred?" asked George.

"I don't know yet. It will depend somewhat on where we are. If we can make Cape Vincent all right we'll have it there."

An hour later John said after he had looked out over the lake, "The wind is getting fresher. Don't you notice it, fellows?"

"Yes," said George. "I hope it will keep it up. I would like to be out here when the Black Growler was rolling a little. I would give a dime to see one of the Go Ahead boys seasick."

"Don't be so extravagant," retorted Fred. "You'll only have a chance to lose your money before night. The wind is rising," he added a moment later.

In the distance the boys saw occasional waves that now were capped with white. The Black Growler also had taken on a rolling motion and although all four of the Go Ahead boys declared that they enjoyed the experience it was noticed after a brief time that Fred was strangely quiet. He was still at the wheel and apparently devoting all his thought to his task.

"Say, fellows, will you take a look at Peewee?" demanded George about ten minutes later. "I believe he is getting sick."

Fred turned and glanced at his companions but did not speak. The color and expression of his face, however, were such as to arouse great elation among his passengers.

"That's the way, Peewee!" laughed John. "You'll have to give up your place at the wheel. I'm sorry that we haven't any doctor on board."

"There was an old fellow down on Long Island Sound," suggested George, "who used to tell us that the best cure for seasickness was a sweet apple and if that wasn't any good then he suggested swallowing a piece of raw salt pork with a string tied to it."

"What was the string for?" demanded John.

"If you can't guess, I shan't tell you," laughed George. "I'm just making these suggestions for little Pyg's benefit. He doesn't look as if he was happy. Hi, Fred!" he added, turning to the pilot, "you had better go back in the stern and lie down."

"I would," answered Fred, who was genuinely miserable now, "if there was any one on board who knew enough to take my place."

"Any one of us can do it," spoke up George glibly.

Fred shook his head in token of his unbelief as he said slowly, "We would go to the bottom."

"We may go there anyway," said John, "if this wind keeps rising. I want you to notice how much higher the waves are and how many more white caps we can see. I don't know what's going to become of us."

The boy spoke seriously and for a moment his companions looked keenly at him.

Sometimes it was difficult to decide just what thoughts were in John's mind. His manner of speaking did not betray his innermost feelings. This time, however, it was evident that he was anxious, if not alarmed, and when a moment later Fred declared that he was so miserable that he must find some relief, the anxiety of the Go Ahead boys increased greatly.

Fred retired to the cockpit and stretched himself at full length upon the cushions of the seats. A ghastly, greenish pallor was upon his face and no proof was required that he was far from being happy.

John now took the wheel and did his utmost to hold the Black Growler to a steady course.

Occasionally the motor-boat was caught in the trough of the waves and the spray dashed over the boys. It was not long before every one was wet, Fred taking more than his full share of the water. He was, however, so miserable that he did not protest and even his friends now were silent as they devoted their efforts to holding the motor-boat steadily to her course.

All thoughts of luncheon were abandoned. Fred, of course, had passed the stage where the thought of food brought any pleasure, while his companions were so busy that they too had forgotten that midday had arrived.

"You don't need to mind this too much," suggested John in his loudest tones. "I have seen the wind come up and then go down just as suddenly as it came. Perhaps that will be the way it will be to-day."

Whatever the thoughts in the minds of George and Grant were they did not express them. They were standing near the wheel eagerly looking before them.

Each boy was hopeful that a boat might be seen which would come to the aid of the unfortunate Black Growler. Several passing steamers were seen low on the horizon, but it was impossible to attract the attention of any.

"I feel," said George at last breaking in upon the silence, "that we made a great mistake this morning when we didn't take the advice of that man in Oswego."

"What man? What was his advice?" asked Grant.

"Why the one who told us that we ought not to start out on Lake Ontario without taking some man along with us who knew the course and could help us if we got into a fix."

"I don't like such remarks at this time," said Grant. "I never want the man who says 'I told you so' to come around to me with his comfort."

"I didn't mean it that way," protested George.

"Of course you didn't, Pop, but we're boxed here as sure as you live. There isn't any use in complaining or in spending our time wishing that we had done something else. Is the wind going down any?"

"Not a bit," spoke up John. "I think it's getting stronger if anything."

Meanwhile the little boat had been rolling and tossing, almost helpless in the trough of the waves. Poor Fred was stretched out at full length on the cushions and the ghastly expression of his face indicated that he at least was not suffering from any fear of the fate which might befall them. He had reached that stage in his sickness wherein he was completely indifferent to his surroundings.

Again and again the anxious boys did their utmost to discover the cause of the trouble. They were unable to find any serious defect with the machinery, however, and their anxiety steadily increased. Several times the motor-boat shipped water and once or twice she was thrown with such violence by the onrushing waves that it did not seem possible she could again right herself.

The boys were now far from land, for only a dim outline of the faraway shore could be seen. They had not taken the direct course to Cape Vincent. Although they might have saved time by doing so, it was considered safer to keep near the shore, although at no place were they within three miles of it.

Another hour elapsed and still the wind continued strong. The sun was shining brightly and the clouds scudding across the face of the sky only occasionally concealed its beams.

The supreme hope in the minds of all had been that their predicament would be discovered and that some one would come to their aid. The shore, however, was so far distant that it was vain to expect help from that direction and on the other hand most of the boats, whose courses were marked by trails of smoke, were so far away that it was almost impossible for them to discern the drifting motor-boat.

CHAPTER XI

RESCUED

No change occurred for another hour in the position in which the boys found themselves. Fred still was lying helpless on the cushions and the boys by taking turns or working together at the wheel had somehow, in spite of numerous moments of peril, been able to keep the Black Growler headed to the wind.

At that time George broke in upon the silence by saying excitedly, "Look yonder, fellows! Isn't that a boat coming this way?"

Instantly the eyes of all three turned in the direction in which George pointed. Far away a trail of smoke was visible and from the direction in which it was moving it was apparent that it had come from a boat which was coming nearer the place where the boys were drifting than had any boats since their mishap.

"I believe it's coming," exclaimed Grant. "We'll get some help pretty soon."

"Yes," broke in John, whose hands now were blistered and whose temper had suffered from his efforts. "Yes, she's probably bound for Liverpool and won't stop until she's gone across the ocean. A lot of good it will do us!"

"Don't take all the joy out of living, String," laughed George good-naturedly. "Maybe we shan't have any chance to be taken on board, but we'll do our best anyway."

Silence followed as the three boys eagerly watched the approaching boat, for there was no question in their minds now that the unknown steamer was approaching.

A few minutes later Grant said, looking through the field glasses at the approaching stranger, "That's a yacht of some kind, in my opinion." As soon as he had spoken, his companions eagerly demanded an opportunity to confirm his statement.

"Soc is right," said John after a long inspection.

"Of course he is," said Grant lightly. "He always is right. How many times must I tell you that if you would only follow my advice you would soon be improving?"

"It's no time to joke," said John solemnly. "We've just got to make them take us on board or help us out of our trouble."

"We'll have to wait until they come nearer than they are now," said George. "Have we got a big white cloth that we can use as a signal?"

"I think there are some sheets down in the cabin," suggested Grant.

"Then I'll get them," said Grant quickly, as he disappeared from sight.

In a brief time he returned with two sheets in his arms. Handing one to Grant, while John was still busy at the wheel, George said excitedly, "Now we have got to stand up and let them know that we're here."

It was plain to the watching boys that the approaching boat was a yacht as Grant had suggested. Her graceful outlines now could be plainly seen and she was swiftly approaching.

"I'm wondering," suggested George thoughtfully, "if we are tossing around on the water the way she is. Just look at her," he added excitedly as the yacht in the distance pitched visibly in the rough water.

"Of course we are," said John, "only worse. A little boat like the Black Growler is not worth much more than an egg shell."

"Still I think I would rather be in the Black Growler," laughed George.

The spray continued to dash over the motor-boat and the little craft was roughly tossed by the passing waves. Fred twice had rolled from his position on the cushions and fallen upon the floor. The assistance of his friends had been required to restore him to his former position. His ghastly appearance by this time had aroused the sympathies of his companions and besides they were all three anxious for the safety of the boat as well as of themselves.

The sun was still shining brightly and there was life in the air as it swept across the great mass of fresh water. Steadily the Black Growler had been moving before the wind, which was blowing directly from the lake.

As a result they were able to see more distinctly the outlines of the shore before them, which now was not more than two miles distant.

A few minutes had elapsed when George said excitedly, "Do you see what boat that is?"

His companions did not reply for a brief time and then Grant said quietly, "It's the Caledonia."

"Yes, I believe it is," joined in John.

"I know it is," said George. "We're sure now that we'll get some help."

"We may have our troubles," suggested Grant, "if the captain answers our hail, or he may pick us up and claim salvage."

"I guess there won't be anything like that," exclaimed George, who was greatly relieved by the sight of the approaching yacht. Her black sides glistened in the sunlight and her graceful outline now that she was near had never appeared to greater advantage.

Two of the boys were still waving and shaking the sheets as their signals of distress. It was evident, however, that they had been seen by the crew of the Caledonia and that the big black yacht was directly bearing down upon them.

A few minutes later the Caledonia shut off steam and the captain was seen on deck.

Approaching the rail, with his speaking trumpet in his hand, he called, "Ahoy, there! What's the trouble?"

"Our engine is broken down," replied John.

"Aren't you the same boys we towed through the Erie Canal yesterday?"

"Yes, sir," replied John.

"You seem to be in trouble most of the way," retorted the captain. "It seems to me the best thing we can do is to take you up and send you back to your mothers. You aren't fit to be out here on Lake Ontario all alone. What do you want us to do?"

At that moment the owner of the yacht again appeared by the captain's side and taking the speaking trumpet from that officer he called to the boys, "Are you in trouble?"

"Yes, sir," replied John, who still was the spokesman for the Go Ahead boys.

"What can we do for you?"

"If you will take us on board, or give us a tow until we can land somewhere we shall be very grateful to you."

"What's the trouble?"

"That's just what we do not know," said John.

"Have you got plenty of gasoline?"

"Yes, sir. It's something wrong with the machinery this time."

Fred now was sitting erect and gazing interestedly at

the people on the deck of the Caledonia. His face was still ghastly in its color but the opportunity to secure help apparently had aroused him from the semi-stupor into which he had fallen.

"I think the best thing will be to take you on board and tow the boat. We're going to put in for the night right here and if there isn't anybody there who can fix up your machinery then you'll have to stay until tomorrow morning when we can take you on to Sacket's Harbor. I think it will be better for all you boys to come aboard," he added. "In a sea like this there's no knowing what may happen to a boat in tow."

"You fellows go on board," said Fred. "I'll stay here and look after the boat."

"You'll do nothing of the kind," retorted John promptly. "If you stay I shall stay with you."

It finally was agreed that the four boys should be taken on board the Caledonia and that one of the crew of the yacht should take his place on board the Black Growler and do his best to see that she was guided aright while she was being towed by the larger boat.

The big yacht was drifting steadily nearer the motorboat and in a brief time it was possible for a rope to be cast. The boys succeeded in making this fast and then the yacht swung around so that the Black Growler was in the lea.

In spite of the rough water the boys succeeded in making their way to the deck of the yacht while one of the crew took his place on board the Black Growler.

The motor-boat then was dropped back and when the Caledonia started, she was fifty feet in the rear of the larger boat.

Mr. Stevens cordially and yet laughingly greeted the boys, whom he dubbed at the time the "sons of misfortune."

Relieved as the Go Ahead boys were by their rescue they nevertheless all showed traces of chagrin over the fact that twice they had been helped by the big, black yacht.

"We're going to put up at Henderson Harbor," explained Mr. Stevens. "I have some friends staying at the big club-house and I have promised to spend the night there. I'm sure there will be a welcome for you boys if you wish to stop. It may be, however, that there will be some one there who can fix you up so that you can go on to Sacket's Harbor if you desire. My suggestion is, however, that you spend the night at the club-house. In the morning we can take your boat in tow again and drop you at Sacket's Harbor or Cape Vincent for such repairs as you may need."

"Thank you," replied John. "I'm sure we shall all be glad to do as you suggest."

At this time the members of Mr. Stevens' family approached the little group and the Go Ahead boys one by one were introduced.

The ghastly expression on the face of Fred in part disappeared when he was introduced to the older daughter of the owner. Miss Susie Stevens laughed in a manner which increased Fred's annoyance when his companions

companions explained the cause of his troubles.

"I wasn't seasick!" declared Fred glibly. "I just had a headache."

"That's all right, Peewee," said George in mock seriousness. "That's all right. All I can say is that if I was not seasick I'm mighty sure I wouldn't be doing some of the things you did."

The young people all laughed at Fred's manifest irritation but the subject was changed, for the Caledonia by this time was drawing near the island on which the club house they were seeking was located.

The water within the harbor was much smoother than on the open lake and the relief from the motion produced by the tossing waves speedily restored Fred so that when at last the yacht was anchored and the Black Growler was safely drawn into the boat house he was ready to take his part with his companions in the events that speedily followed.

CHAPTER XII

A BATTLE WITH ARMS AND LEGS

The Go Ahead boys enjoyed a bath in the lake before they reported at the club-house in response to the invitation of Mr. Stevens. Even Fred had now thoroughly recovered from his experience and was more than positive that he had not been seasick. His strong words greatly delighted his friends, who aware now that he was sensitive concerning the matter, lost no opportunity to describe his sufferings which began soon after they set sail from Oswego.

At first the boys had insisted that as soon as the difficulty with the Black Growler had been remedied they must proceed at once on their way. When it was found, however, that there was no mechanic at the club-house they were easily persuaded to abandon their project and accept the hospitality of Mr. Stevens for the night.

Early the following morning a man skilled in all the uncertain ways of motor-boats arrived in response to the summons of the officials and in a brief time he discovered that there was nothing seriously wrong with the Black Growler. Indeed, within a few minutes he was racing the swift little motor-boat over the waters of Lake Ontario, which now was calm once more.

The club-house was located on an island at the entrance of a marvelously beautiful harbor. Three miles inland and about an equal number in length the waters appeared like a great bowl. High wooded shores were seen on one shore and on another a row of attractive cottages behind which the road was visible winding in and out in the direction of Sacket's Harbor.

Soon after breakfast, when Fred declared that it was time for the Go Ahead boys to start; Mr. Stevens said, "I think you young gentlemen will do well to take Sam Hodge along with you. He's an excellent mechanic and if anything goes wrong he will know what to do."

"How about Fred?" demanded George, whose eyes twinkled as he spoke. "Can he fix him up if he is seasick again?"

"I'm not going to be seasick," retorted Fred. "I wasn't seasick yesterday. I have told you so ten times."

Ignoring the protest, George said, "It seems to me it ought to be as easy to adjust the internal workings of Peewee as those of the Black Growler. Perhaps a dose of a similar kind might be good for both. "George's face was expressionless and his voice did not betray his purpose of bantering his diminutive friend.

Fred's face flushed an angry red, for Miss Susie Stevens and other members of the club were standing on the dock when the conversation occurred. Her black eyes twinkled with mischief and it was manifest that she was enjoying the visit of the boys.

"I think," said Grant positively, "that we had better take Sam Hodge with us. We ought to arrive at your grandfather's place by night, Fred, and he can come back by train."

"That's right. That's right," spoke up John quickly. "I had to steer the Black Growler most of the time yesterday and my arms are lame."

"All the length of them?" asked George. "Why, think when John has a pain how long he must have it."

John turned quickly upon his tormentor as he said, "That's the thirteenth time I have heard you get off that old joke. You mustn't take him too seriously, Miss Susie," he added, turning to the girl, who was laughing at George 's suggestion. "You know what his nickname is, don't you?"

"No, I cannot say that I do," replied Miss Susie.

"Well, we call him Pop."

"Why?" she inquired.

"Because he's the papa of his country. He is named for George Washington, who is the Father of his Country, but the name doesn't go very far."

"That's all right," spoke up George. "Up yonder where your topknot is there's an aching void. I read the other day that Sydney Smith said 'Nature never built a man more than seven stories high without leaving the top loft empty'."

"On the contrary," spoke up John, "all the great men have been those who could look down on the rest of the world."

"Huh!" broke in Grant, "it will do you good to find out how much of your statement is really true. What do you think of Caesar, Napoleon, William of Orange, General Grant, Alexander Stephens, Alexander Hamilton -"

"That will do, my son. That will do," said John, patting Grant upon the head. "That is a sufficiency of information this morning. Pray desist. In other words, shut up. If we don't stop you pretty soon you'll start in on the matter of canals again. All the way up from New York," he added, turning to Miss Susie as he spoke, "he has been giving us undigested and undesirable information about the canals. He even said that the Amsterdam Canal connected the Zuider Zee with the North Sea."

"So it does," said Grant quickly. "If you'll tell me how long that canal is I'll buy the dinner, when we stop at Cape Vincent."

"One hundred and sixty-five miles," declared John promptly. As he spoke, however, he glanced at his cuff on which the fact was plainly written.

"That doesn't count," declared Grant. "No ponying in this game. Look up into the sky, John, which isn't very far from you, and if you'll tell me how long the Panama Canal is I'll call it square and buy the dinner."

"The - Panama - Canal - is - is - quite long."

"So I have heard," laughed Grant. "I guess you buy the dinner."

"How long is it?" inquired John. "I knew, but I have forgotten."

"It's fifty and one-half miles long. Here comes Sam Hodge," Grant added as the boatman came alongside the dock. "Are you going with us?" he inquired as he quickly approached the dock.

"Where's that?" inquired Sam.

"Down the St. Lawrence River."

"How far?"

"Oh, down among the Thousand Islands, that's all."

"First I have heard of it," said Sam.

"I think it will be a good thing if you can go with the boys, Sam," spoke up Mr. Stevens. "They had a mishap yesterday and didn't quite know what to do."

"Sure, I'll go," said Sam.

Fred made no protests and the terms with the mechanic were speedily arranged.

A half-hour later the Black Growler set forth on her voyage.

The Caledonia was to follow some time that day and plans already had been made by which the boys were to spend some time on Hecla Island, on which was located the summer home of the Stevens.

Fortunately for Fred, at least, the lake continued to be

calm. In the eagerness of the boy to prove to his friends that he merely had a "headache" the preceding day and had not been seasick, he was unusually busy.

Sam called the attention of the Go Ahead boys to the post at Sacket's Harbor. On a bluff above the lake the barracks and other buildings of the place were plainly visible. Even the soldiers stationed there could be plainly seen as they moved about the quarters.

"That's a great place to have an army post," said George. "I can't think of any place better unless it's in the middle of the Sahara Desert. Why did the government establish a post here?"

"Because there was a fort here, 'way back in the War of 1812," answered Grant promptly. "Sacket's Harbor was the headquarters of the army of the North and so the place has been kept up ever since."

"Do any of you want to stop?" inquired Fred, glancing at his companions as he spoke.

"Not I," replied John quickly. "When we have a good sea like this and Fred can be safe from the misery he suffered yesterday I'm not for taking any chances of the wind coming up later."

"That's mighty kind of you," growled Fred. "I never knew you to be so thoughtful of any one, - except yourself."

"Don't say that," said John. "You don't mean it. What you mean is that this is the first time you ever have appreciated how good I am."

"Huh," began Fred in response. His reply, however, was interrupted by Sam Hodge as he said, "This is a mighty good boat. She must have cost a pile of money."

"She did," said George quickly. "Fred had to save up his spending money for several days before he bought her. You don't talk like a native around here, Sam. Where did you come from?"

"I come from New York," answered Sam.

"What were you doing there?"

"Oh, I worked in a factory where we made legs and feet and arms for dummies and models."

"Fine job," laughed George. "Did you like it?"

"I liked the job all right," replied Sam, "but I didn't like our foreman. I quit on account of him."

"What was wrong with him?"

"Everything," said Sam quietly.

"So that was why you left and came up here to work on motor-boats was it?"

"Yes," answered Sam. "That foreman was the hardest man to get along with I ever saw. I put up with it for months, but finally there came a day when I decided I wouldn't stand any more of it."

"What happened?"

"Why, I had a sore hand and I asked him to cut one of my feet off and he cut it off for me and then he got mad at something I said and threw one of his legs at me. Then not satisfied with that he took one of the girl's feet and threw that at me, too. Of course I got mad. I picked up one of my legs in my hand and I tried to defend myself and then he hit me in the eye with one of his hands and knocked me over among a lot of legs and arms. He almost broke my foot and -"

"Did you say he cut one of your feet off?" asked Grant, soberly looking down at the pedal extremities of the mechanic, as he did so.

"That's just what he did," answered Sam.

"But it seems to be all right now," protested Fred.

"You don't quite see," said Sam. "I'm talking about the foreman of the factory where I worked over on Broome Street. We manufactured legs and feet and arms for dummies and models like I was telling you."

"Like those that we see in the show windows?"

"That's it exactly," said Sam. "Those dummies and models that they put in the store windows to display gowns on. I was working on one of the artificial feet and I mean he broke it. Oh, no, he didn't cut one of my REAL feet off. But he did hit me in the eye with one of his hands."

"I see," said George seriously. "It was an artificial eye of yours that he hit."

"No, it wasn't," retorted Sam. "It was my real eye."

"But he hit it with one of his artificial hands. Is that it, or did he hit it with one of the hands he manufactured?"

"No. No," said Sam. "He hit me in my real eye with his real hand."

"And that was why you picked up one of your legs and he took one of the girl's feet and he hit you in the real eye, no, I mean the artificial eye with his real hand, - that's not quite it. I mean he hit you in the hand with his artificial eye. No, that isn't it either. Hold on. He threw one of his legs at you and then he took his eye and threw it at one of the girl's feet. Hold on, I'm getting all mixed up. I can't tell just where I am at. Say it again, Sam."

"I think it's better for a man to have a wooden leg than it is to have a wooden head," spoke up Fred.

"Splendid, Peewee! Fine!" laughed George. "That's immense! Great! Sam," he added soberly as he turned to the mechanic who was now steering the Black Growler, "did you say you made artificial legs and arms and feet?"

"That's what I said," acknowledged Sam.

"Did you ever manufacture artificial heads?"

"Lots of 'em. Lots of 'em."

"Have you got any with you?"

"No, I haven't."

"I'm sorry," said George. "There are several reasons why I should like to buy one."

Meanwhile the Black Growler swiftly and greatly to the delight of Sam was speeding over the smooth waters. Scarcely a ripple was to be seen. The reflection of the sunlight increased the discomfort of the Go Ahead boys and all four were rejoiced when at last Cape Vincent was sighted in the distance.

CHAPTER XII

A SURPRISE

"Wait a minute, fellows!" called Fred when his companions prepared to depart from the dock and go to the hotel for their luncheon. "I have lost my knife. I think I must have dropped it somewhere behind the cushions."

The boys halted on the dock while Fred speedily turned over the cushions. He did not discover his missing knife, but he did find a large envelope lying directly beneath the cushion in the stern of the cockpit.

"What's that?" he called as he held the paper up to view. "Have any of you fellows lost anything?"

All three Go Ahead boys declared that the paper did not belong to any of them. Approaching the place where Fred was standing on board and still looking at the document Grant suggested that he should open the envelope as it was unsealed and unaddressed.

Fred followed the suggestion and to the amazement as well as to the consternation of his friends he drew forth a bond for five thousand dollars. For a moment an expression of blank amazement appeared on the faces of all on board.

"What's that?" demanded Fred at last. "Whose is it? What is it doing on board the Black Growler?"

"It's a railway mortgage bond and given by one of the strongest railroads in the United States," said Grant, who had been looking carefully at the surprising discovery which his friend had made.

"Is it good for anything?" inquired John.

"Not much," laughed Grant. "Only five thousand dollars, that's all."

"Do you mean to tell me you could get five thousand dollars for that piece of paper?"

"Yes, sir, I think you could."

"Well, then," said John, "why don't we do it? It may be as good as money, as you say, but I think I'd rather see the cold cash. Where can we get the money?"

"It might take a little time to get it cashed, but almost any bank would pay it. It's not a registered bond and it looks as if it was all right every way."

"Yes, but whose is it?" said Fred. "That's what troubles me."

"I guess you won't have any trouble in finding out whose bond it is," laughed George. "Though I must confess I don't see how it came on board."

"Neither do I," said Fred slowly. "It must have been here some time."

"Yes," said John dryly. "I guess this is the first time we have turned over or shaken out the cushions."

"'We' have shaken out, is good," retorted Fred. "I was doing this little job all myself. There wasn't a fellow who offered to lend a hand. But what shall I do with the thing?" he added.

"Put it in your pocket now," said Grant, "and wait until we have had our luncheon. We can talk it over while we are at the table and decide what is the best thing to do."

Grant's advice was followed. Fred thrust the bond into the envelope and then placed the package in the inner pocket of his jacket.

Throughout their meal the discovery of the bond was the chief topic of conversation. The mystery of its presence on board the Black Growler as well as that of its ownership again and again were talked over, but no satisfactory conclusion had been obtained when at last the boys departed from the hotel.

"I'll tell you what we'll do, fellows," said Grant. "Let's take that bond down to the bank. There must be one or two banks here and we can find out about it and leave it there, if it is thought best. It may be that we shan't want to be found with the goods on us a little later."

"That's all right, Soc," said Fred, who was more nervous than any of the boys concerning the discovery which he had made. "I'll find out where there's a bank."

In response to his inquiries, Fred soon was informed where a bank could be found and together with his companions at once entered it.

He inquired for the president and soon was introduced to that official. Briefly Fred then related the story of the discovery of the bond. The man before him listened attentively and when Fred ceased he said, "Let me see the bond."

As soon as he received it he carefully read its contents and then said slowly, "That is a perfectly good bond and is worth at least fifty-two hundred and fifty dollars. What do you intend to do with it?"

"That's what we wanted to ask you," explained Fred.

"And you haven't any idea where it came from?" inquired the banker, looking keenly at Fred as he spoke.

"Not the slightest," answered Fred. "I never was more surprised in my life than when I found that bond under the cushion on our boat."

"Hum," said the banker slowly. "Will you accept a suggestion from me?"

"Yes, sir," said Fred eagerly. "That's what we came for."

"Then my advice to you is to leave the bond here. I'll give you a description of it and the number, and will make such inquiries as are in my power concerning its ownership. You must give me your names and addresses and tell me where I can get you on the 'phone within the next few days if I want to call you."

Fred glanced questioningly at his companions and when Grant nodded his head, he said, "All right Mr. -"

"My name is Reese," explained the banker.

"All right, Mr. Reese," said Fred. "You give us the paper and we'll be glad to leave the bond here in your keeping. Have you any idea," he added, "how that bond may have been placed on board our boat?"

"No, sir, not the slightest," replied the banker.

Mr. Reese retired from the room in which the boys were waiting and in a moment returned stating that as soon as the chief facts concerning the bond had been transcribed he would give a copy to the boys. Meanwhile he took the names of all four Go Ahead boys and also their addresses.

"I know your grandfather quite well," he explained when Fred gave his name as that in the care of which all letters and messages for the boys should be sent. "He frequently comes up to Cape Vincent in his yacht. I am glad to meet you on his account as well as on your own."

The task at last having been completed, the Go Ahead boys at once started toward the dock where their motor-boat had been left.

As they drew near the place, John suddenly stopped and clutching George by his arm, who was walking beside him, said, "Look at that man over on the dock! Who is it?"

"It's the fellow who was the leader of that gang of canal-men that boarded us the other morning."

"What do you suppose he's doing here?" demanded

John in a whisper.

"I can't say. I'm not sure that it is the same man, but it certainly looks like him."

The boys stopped and excitedly explained to their friends the discovery which they had made.

The opinion was general as soon as all had looked at the man that it was indeed their unwelcome visitor who had fled precipitately with his companions when the Caledonia had stopped to aid them.

The stranger was only a few yards from the place where the Black Growler had been made fast, and as the boys approached he looked up and said with a laugh, "Glad to see yer. I thought I'd come down and look ye up. I wonder if yer got any gasoline?"

"Yes, sir, we have," answered Fred tartly. He was not desirous of continuing the conversation.

Sam Hodge, who had come with the boys from Henderson Harbor, had departed soon after the landing at Cape Vincent had been made. Consequently the Black Growler had been left without any one on board when the Go Ahead boys had gone to the hotel for their luncheon. Whether or not the man before them had made investigations or helped himself to anything of value on board the boat no one knew. There was, however, no one to prevent him from doing such things as he had desired.

"Where did you come from?" demanded George as he stepped in front of the stranger.

"I jes' started for me summer home," laughed the canal-man. "I didn't think I would go down before the Fourth of July, but the sight of you boys made me homesick."

"Where is your island?"

"I can't jes' describe it," said the man, "but if you'll give me a lift in your boat I'll p'int it out to you when we come to it."

"How did you come down here?" demanded George.

"The same as any gintleman might come. I thought of comin' in me yacht, but I finally decided I'd take me own car and in that way I would be indepindent of the whole world. Now, then, boys," he added, "I'm a bit fearful that I shan't be able to stay with ye very long. Did any of ye find a document of any value after I left ye the other day? I was a bit sorry I couldn't stop to shake hands with ye, but there were several reasons why me and me pals thought it might be a good thing not to interfere with you when your friends on that black yacht stopped to say good mornin'."

The four boys looked shyly at one another, every one of them convinced that the mystery of the presence of the bond which they had discovered was in part explained.

"What was your document?" asked Grant.

"That wasn't what I said," replied the man. "I asked you if you had found any document."

"Of course we'd find a good many things on board,"

explained Grant. "You'll have to tell us just what it is you lost, if you want us to say whether or not we have found it."

"You found it all the same. I can see it by the look in your eyes," declared the man. "Now, what I want to know is if you'll give it up peaceable-like or do you want me to call a policeman and get him to help me take what belongs to me."

CHAPTER XIV

A SURPRISING PASSENGER

"We haven't got your bond," said Fred quickly. He was somewhat uneasy as he was aware when he glanced keenly at the man that he was unusually strong and if he really had obtained possession of the security in a way that was open to suspicion it was quite probable that he would not hesitate to defend what he had taken.

Fred glanced anxiously about the dock to ascertain if help was near in case it should be required.

"Where is it?" demanded the stranger.

"We found it on the boat."

"Yes, I know you did," interrupted the man, "but what I want is for you to let me see it or tell me where it is."

"I tell you we haven't got it," said Fred.

"Where is it?"

"It's where it will be safe until it can be looked up and we find out whose it is."

"Where did you get that bond?" demanded George,

abruptly breaking in upon the conversation.

"Did I say it was mine?" demanded the stranger.

"You asked for it."

"If I recall, I asked about it."

"That's the same thing," retorted George.

"Not quite," said the man. "Now then, will you tell me where it is?"

"I don't think we shall," spoke up Fred. "If you'll tell me who owns it and what it was doing on our motor-boat, then perhaps I'll be willing to talk with you."

"Then you say you'll not tell me where it is?" said the man, speaking slowly and looking savagely at Fred as he spoke.

"I shan't tell you," said Fred. "Now, if you're done, we'll start."

As he spoke, Fred stepped on board the Black Growler, an action which was speedily followed by his companions. Advancing to the wheel Fred inspected everything to satisfy himself that all things were in readiness for their departure and then said to the man waiting on the dock, "We'll have to bid you good-by."

At the same time he turned on the power. As George and John pushed the little boat out from the dock it began to move, but not before the canal-man unbidden suddenly leaped on board.

"Thank you for your very kind invitation," he said as he seated himself on the cushions.

"We didn't ask you to come," spoke up Fred, "and we don't want your company. You'll have to go ashore."

"Is that so?" laughed the man banteringly.

"Yes, sir, it's so!" retorted Fred.

"Well, then if I go ashore I think there will be some-body going with me."

"You're mistaken," said Fred. "We're going down among the Thousand Islands."

"That doesn't make any difference to me. I'm going to find out who took that bond. If you don't tell me where it is then I shall go to a constable or justice and get out a warrant for you. You have owned up that you had the bond on board your boat. It was a stolen bond and I have been trying to run it down for some time. Now I have found it, or at least I have found the party that had it, and you try to bluff me by saying that you won't tell me where it is. Now, I'll give you your choice. You can have my company, for I shan't leave you until I find out more about it, or you can try to put me ashore and I'll get help. Just as sure as you're sitting here I'll swear out a warrant and have you arrested for stealing that bond."

The boys were inexperienced and for a moment they stared blankly at one another, startled more than they were willing to acknowledge by the bold threat of their unwelcome passenger.

"Well, what is it?" said the man a moment later when no reply had been given to his questions. "Which do you want?"

"The thing for us to do," said Grant in a low voice to Fred, "is to keep right on. We'll take this man down to your grandfather's island and when we get there we'll tell him all about it. He'll know best what to do and we'll wait for his advice before we do anything."

"That's all right, Soc," said Fred, greatly relieved by the words of his friend. Then turning to their passenger he said more boldly than before he had spoken, "I guess we'll take our chances and have you go with us. We'll find out more about this later and give you a chance to tell your story."

"It's all the same to me," said the man glibly. "I'll be glad to have the ride anyway. It's been a long time since I have been on the St. Lawrence River."

Apparently Fred's threat had produced slight effect upon the addition to their party. He spoke as if he were in no fear for himself, while his threat to swear out a warrant for the boys, although it had startled them, had not greatly alarmed any one.

Meanwhile the Black Growler, almost as if she was sharing in the excitement of the boys, was speeding swiftly down the river. The broad expanse of water when she left her dock at Cape Vincent soon was broken by the sight of many islands, some of which were miles in extent while others were tiny little spots, just lifted above the surface of the water.

There was some anxiety on the part of John, that,

unfamiliar as they were with the channel, they might strike some hidden rock, but Fred assured his friend that there was slight danger of that in the daytime, as a careful watch was maintained and it was easy for them to follow the course of boats that were in advance of them.

"Look yonder!" said George, suddenly pointing as he spoke to a yacht that was swiftly approaching from the Canadian side of the river.

"Do you know what boat that is?" exclaimed John.

"We ought to know it," said Fred. "That's the Varmint II."

"She beat us down here by a good deal," suggested George, who was keenly observing the graceful and swift little motor-boat that was steadily approaching.

"I don't know about that," retorted Fred. "She may be just coming now."

"Don't you believe it," retorted George. "She has been here a long time and they're just out testing her on the river. Are you going to try to race with her here?"

"I am not," retorted Fred promptly. "It will be time enough when we see what she can do in the real race. That won't be for three weeks yet."

"How many races do they have down here in the summer?" inquired John.

"I don't know," answered Fred. "Two, I guess."

"One will be enough this summer, I'm thinking," laughed John. "What are we going to do with that man?" As he spoke John glanced again at the uninvited and unwelcome passenger who apparently was taking his ease on the cushions in the stern of the boat.

"I'm going to do nothing," said Fred quickly. "I think I will leave him alone until we land at my grandfather's island and then I will tell him all about it."

"What do you suppose he is?" inquired John, glancing again at the man, who apparently was unaware of the interest his presence on board the Black Growler had aroused.

"I haven't any idea."

"How did he know about that bond?"

"I can't tell you."

"Do you suppose he stole it?"

"It doesn't seem so to me," said Fred slowly, as he shook his head. "If he stole it I can't understand why he comes down here after it. You would think he would want to put a long distance between himself and that bond after he lost it."

"And yet he seemed bold enough when he told us to tell him where it is. What do you suppose made him think of that?"

"Think of what?"

"Why, that we had put it somewhere."

"It's the most natural thing in the world," retorted Fred glibly. "He would know that fellows like us wouldn't want to keep a bond of that size. I am wondering what it all means."

"First thing you know that man will jump on us all and take the Black Growler away from us. I tell you he's a desperate character. Just look at those hands. If he had his coat off I tell you you would see the muscles of his shoulders stand out like great knots. He's a powerful brute and I don't like his disposition. I wish he was somewhere else."

"I guess he wouldn't attack us," laughed Fred. "We're four to one and even if he's stronger than any one of us he's not as strong as all four of us put together."

"I tell you," said John more positively, "he's a pirate. He's a regular pirate. He stole that bond and tried to take the motor-boat away from us when we were on the canal and I shall feel mighty well satisfied if he doesn't get it away from us now before we go very much farther."

"I confess it's all mighty queer, John, but I don't believe the man will attack us. He has got too many matters just now to look after to try such a fool thing as that."

"But I can't understand why he forces himself on board and why he insists on going with us down the river. I shouldn't be surprised to have him stop us when we are in some quiet place and search the boat. How does he know that the bond isn't here?"

"Because he has searched the Black Growler already,"

replied Fred. "You may be sure he has gone through every nook and cranny before we came back from the bank."

"I guess you're right," assented John, as once more he glanced apprehensively at the man who was the subject of their conversation.

"I don't know of but one way to get even with him," suggested Fred.

"What's that?"

"Why, to set Soc on him and make him answer questions about canals. I'm telling you that if Grant should ask him about how wide the Suez Canal is or how deep the Sault Ste. Marie is he'd get an answer that would surprise him."

"I haven't any doubt about that," said John somewhat ruefully. "The man is a surprise anyway."

John spoke more truly than he knew. The surprise that was occasioned by the presence of their unbidden guest was mild compared with that which soon followed.

CHAPTER XV

AN UPSET

The Black Growler, carried forward by the current of the mighty river as well as by her own power, brought the party on board to their destination late in the afternoon.

It was the first time that Fred's friends had seen the spot. The clear running water of the great river, the skies without a cloud, the sight of the numberless camps and cottages, as well as of the many yachts and motor-boats that were to be seen on the river, all combined to increase the interest of the Go Ahead boys.

When at last they arrived at the island owned by Fred's grandfather their enthusiasm became still greater. A beautiful cottage, which really was a house with twenty rooms, was located in a grove of high trees. The boathouse, ample and attractive in every way, and the sight of several skiffs that had been made fast to the dock caused George to exclaim in his impulsive manner, "There isn't a place like it in all the world! I never saw such a spot before in all my life!"

"But you're young yet," suggested Grant soberly.

"But I have seen some things, even if I am young," retorted George. "I thought Mackinac Island was beautiful, but this has some things you can't find up there."

"Spoken like a philosopher," again retorted John. The expression on his face was serious as he hastily made inquiries concerning Grant's missing bag. "The poor chap," he explained, "is in trouble. He can't wear any clothes that fit the rest of us and unless he gets help soon we shall have to lock him in the boathouse for he won't be presentable anywhere."

To Grant's delight his bag already was in his room awaiting his coming. The mistake had occurred at Albany which had caused as much trouble to the owner of the other bag as Grant himself had suffered.

As soon as the boys were ready they all went down to the broad piazza which adjoined the house on three sides and there were greeted cordially by Fred's grandfather and grandmother.

"We're always glad to see Freddie," said Mrs. Button, beaming affectionately upon her grandson, as she spoke, "and you may be sure that his friends are all as welcome as he is."

"Thank you, Mrs. Button," said George promptly. "If you knew how glad we are to be here you might feel almost as if you were doing missionary work in inviting us."

"She will think she's doing missionary work, I'm afraid," spoke up Grant. "I want to warn you, Mrs. Button, that when George gets into the dining room you'll have to drive him out. It's the only way we can get him to stop."

Mrs. Button smiled as she said, "That's just the kind of a guest I like."

Meanwhile Fred had not been with his companions when they had gone to their rooms, for he had remained behind to talk with his grandfather concerning the uninvited passenger who had arrived with them.

"Yes," Fred explained, "he was with some other men, canal-men we thought they were, that boarded us between Utica and Rome and we couldn't get rid of them. I thought at first they were going to try to take the Black Growler away from us, but they didn't do that and when Mr. Stevens came along in the Caledonia and stopped to help us they all ran away. We didn't think that we would ever see any of them again, but up here at Cape Vincent who should show up but this man."

"What did he come for?" inquired Mr. Button. "We couldn't understand it at first," replied Fred, "but, Grandfather, we found under a cushion a bond for five thousand dollars."

"You did what?"

"We found a bond for five thousand dollars."

"What kind of a bond was it?"

"I don't know," said Fred somewhat foolishly. "I know it was a railroad bond."

"What did you do with it?"

"We took it to the bank in Cape Vincent. We left it there with the man who is in charge."

"Did you get a receipt for it?"

"Yes, sir."

"That's right. That's right," said Mr. Button, nodding his head approvingly. "Go on."

"Well, when we came back from the bank whom should we find on board our motor-boat but this same man, that we had seen on the Erie Canal. He demanded that we should give up the bond."

"So he knew about the bond, did he?"

"So it seemed. But we told him we didn't have it. Then he wanted to know what we had done with it and we wouldn't tell him. When we wanted him to go ashore he wouldn't do it, and just stayed on board and said he was coming with us. I thought it was better to let him come -"

"That was kind of you," broke in his grandfather, with a smile.

"I thought it was better to let him come and turn him over to you to deal with than it was for us to have any trouble up there at Cape Vincent."

"That's all right, Fred," said his grandfather. "I'll go right down there and talk with him."

Fred watched his grandfather as he started toward the dock and then he quickly entered the house and went to his room.

A half-hour later when he returned to the piazza and joined his friends who already were seated there, his grandfather, bidding him follow him to the library, said as soon as the door was closed behind them, "What about that bond?"

"I told you all I know."

"You say it was a five thousand dollar bond?"

"Yes, sir."

"And a railroad bond?"

"Yes, sir."

"Do you remember which road?"

"Yes, sir. It was the New York Central."

"But you don't know what kind of a bond?"

"No, sir. I didn't know there was more than one kind."

"Perhaps you'll know more about that later," replied Mr. Button dryly.

"Did this man that came with us know anything more than we did about it?"

Ignoring the question Mr. Button said, "Your friend has gone."

"Who? The man we brought with us?"

"Yes. I had Tom take him over to Alexandria Bay in the Jessie."

"And where is he going?" inquired Fred astounded by the statement of his grandfather.

"He will go to Syracuse. Whether he will stay there or not I do not know."

"But what did he say?" asked Fred somewhat impatiently. "Do you think he stole the bond?"

"There are a good many things that are somewhat strange connected with this affair. I am quite inclined to think your bond is good. About this man, there are some matters that must be cleared up before I can make any explanations to you." Rising as he spoke Mr. Button led the way back to the piazza and Fred was convinced that it was useless for him to talk any more, for the present at least, about the man or the bond.

The following morning the four Go Ahead boys set forth in the Black Growler on a voyage on the river. Fred was eager to show the wonders of the great St. Lawrence to his friends and equally desirous of trying out the motor-boat.

In the time which was to intervene before the race was held he was eager to make himself familiar with every feature of the marvelous little craft. All things were novel and interesting to his companions, both in the scenery through which they were passing and the detailed parts of the Black Growler.

"My grandfather says," exclaimed Fred, "that if we want to we can send over to Henderson Harbor and perhaps can get Sam Hodge to come here. He will be a good man to have on board when we are in that race. I never saw any one that knew more about machinery than he did."

"I'm telling you that you're still youthful," remarked Grant. "Your experience is very limited."

"That may be so," acknowledged Fred with a laugh, "but it's something I'll get over."

"Look yonder!" broke in John. "There's the Varmint II ahead of us. I wonder if you can catch up with her!" As he spoke, John turned and winked slowly at George who at once advanced to Fred's side.

"Of course I can catch her if I want to," declared Fred.

"Which means that if you don't want to you can't catch her," laughed John derisively. "I don't believe there's anything you want more than to catch up with her."

"I can do it," said Fred.

"That's easy to say."

Irritated by the laughter of his companions, who were eager to test the swiftness of their boat, Fred at once turned on more power and the Black Growler instantly responded.

The boat seemed almost to sink a foot or more into the water as she plowed her way up the river.

In a brief time the crew of the Varmint II were aware of the swiftly approaching boat, but instead of entering into the contest they did not increase their speed. In a few minutes the Black Growler swiftly passed the Varmint II and as they did so George said mockingly, "Splendid! Splendid, Fred. All you need is to have the other boat stand still and you can win out every time."

"I gave her every chance," retorted Fred.

"May be you did," answered George, "but she didn't think it wasworth while to take up your challenge."

"She didn't dare to," spoke up John, who was loyal to his friend.

"That all may be so," laughed George derisively. There was nothing he enjoyed more than teasing Fred and as this was a comparatively easy matter it is not surprising that he frequently engaged in the task.

Meanwhile the Black Growler swept onward in her course, at last starting on her return voyage. Not far from the island owned by Fred's grandfather was another island which the boys already had been informed had been rented by Mr. Stevens for the summer.

When Fred pointed out the spot his companions were at once interested and suggested that he should stop at the dock, which almost seemed to invite their coming.

"There's Susie Stevens now," called John, pointing as he spoke to a nearby canoe in which two young girls were seated. One of them was paddling, while her companion was seated in the opposite end of the frail little craft.

At the moment of John's discovery apparently Miss Susie also became aware of the approach of the Black Growler. As she lifted her paddle to salute the Go Ahead boys, her companion, who doubtless was unfamiliar with canoes, reached forward to pick up a sweater to wave at the motor-boat; she suddenly destroyed the balance of the little canoe. Instantly it was overturned and both girls were thrown into the St. Lawrence.

CHAPTER XVI

THE RESCUE

A cry of horror and alarm arose from the startled boys when they beheld the accident. In a moment one of the girls was seen swimming near the overturned canoe. The other, however, was not within sight.

"It's time for us to do something!" shouted John, who was almost beside himself in his excitement.

Fred at once had changed the course of the Black Growler but a semi-circle was necessary to be turned before she could approach the place where the girls had fallen into the river.

Grant, meanwhile promptly had removed his sweater and taken off his sneakers preparing to go to the assistance of the unfortunate girls. As he was the strongest and swiftest swimmer, his companions by common consent had expected him to be the one to leap into the water.

A moment later it was seen that one of the girls had seized the canoe. In her desperation, however, the frail little craft was over-turned and she lost her hold and again disappeared from sight.

At that moment the motor-boat approached within twenty-five feet of the place where the accident had occurred. Shouting to his friends to take the canoe and do their utmost to rescue the unfortunate girl, Grant dived from the deck of the Black Growler and a moment later with powerful strokes was swiftly approaching the victims of the accident.

Meanwhile, following the instructions of Grant, John and George had been able with a boat-hook to reach the overturned canoe and drawing it speedily to them, both carefully and hastily took their places on board.

"Get one of the girls while I am getting the other," called Grant as he turned his head for a moment toward his companions.

At that instant Grant saw the face of one of the girls appear on the surface but a moment later it again disappeared from sight.

The current was moderately strong, and aware that when she again was seen it would be a little farther down the river, Grant slowly moved with the stream.

The depth of the water made it impossible for him to dive in an effort to find her in the depths. Carefully he scanned the water all about him and when in a brief time her face once more was seen and only a few feet farther down the stream, with two powerful strokes he darted forward and succeeded in seizing the girl by the hair of her head just as she began to sink once more.

Grant was elated when he discovered that the girl was still conscious. Holding to her hair with one hand he contrived to place himself behind her. Then holding her up by one hand with which he grasped her under the shoulder, he said hastily, "Don't move. Don't try to do anything for yourself. There, don't do that," he added as the frantic girl made an effort to seize him. "Don't touch me. Keep just as you are and you'll be all right."

In a measure his orders were obeyed. Instead of trying to swim toward the boat Grant was simply doing his utmost to keep himself and his companion afloat. He was treading water and moving with the current.

At the same time he looked all about him for help. He saw two of his friends in the canoe and was relieved when he discovered that John, who in his excitement had neglected to drop the boat-hook was holding the long implement toward the other girl who already had grasped it with both hands and was being drawn toward the boys.

"Come here and help me," shouted Grant. He was hoping that his two friends would be able to rescue the other girl, or at least prevent her from sinking, but he was well aware that if he and his companion were to be saved help soon must be had.

In response to his hail Fred turned the bow of the Black Growler and slowly approached the place where Grant was struggling.

The girl now was motionless and Grant's great anxiety was in a measure relieved. He had been fearful that she would try to seize him by the neck or arms and prevent him from doing anything to help either of them.

Grant was aware also that his strength would not

permit him to continue the struggle much longer. Already he was breathing heavily and all his powers were required to keep himself and the nearly unconscious girl afloat. He had been able thus far to hold her head above the water, for fortunately at this time the river was unusually calm.

Again, almost in despair, he looked back at the motorboat.

"Here!" called Fred, who had left the wheel and was standing in the bow holding a rope in his hand. "Catch this!" He had hastily tied a noose in the end and as he threw this toward the struggling boy, Grant fortunately grasped it.

By a supreme effort he managed to slip one arm through the noose and as soon as this had been done Fred instantly began to pull. Several times in spite of all the care Fred was exercising, the heads of Grant and his companion were drawn beneath the water. Still Grant managed to maintain his hold upon the girl and in a brief time they were drawn alongside the Black Growler.

"I can't pull you both up," called Fred in his excitement.

"No," gasped Grant. "I don't think you can pull either one of us."

While he was speaking he had contrived to slip the noose over the shoulders and under the arms of his companion. As soon as this had been done, he released his hold and said to Fred, "You can keep her head out of the water anyway. If your noose holds she's all right."

"What are you going to do?" demanded Fred.

"I'm all right," responded Grant as turning himself upon his back he floated with the current and obtained a brief rest.

Meanwhile John and George had drawn Miss Susie Stevens to the canoe and seized her by her hands. John had been seated in the stern but now he stretched himself upon the bottom of the little craft and reached over with his hands, one on each side of the canoe, and held the girl up so that she was able to breathe, although he did not attempt to draw her out of the water. "Take your paddle," he called to George. "I've got her all right, but make for the Black Growler. There's no knowing what will happen."

In this manner the canoe slowly was paddled toward the motor-boat, but Fred was holding the rope by which the second girl was held and consequently was unable to respond to the appeal of his friends to come to their aid.

Meanwhile the motor-boat was drifting with the current and there was grave danger that she might run aground on some one of the numerous islands.

Indeed this was just what occurred a few minutes later.

The keel of the boat now grated on the rocky bottom. Grant, who had been following the same course now obtained a precarious foothold and at once advanced to the aid of the helpless girl. He was still breathing heavily from his own exertions and his strength had not fully returned. Stumbling, slipping on the rocks, twice nearly falling into the river he managed to draw the girl up on the shore and as soon as he was satisfied that she was living he called to Fred, "Go on back and help the other fellows and I'll run up to this cottage and get some one to look after this girl."

"Give me a push, I'm almost grounded," called Fred frantically.

The engine had been reversed and the added help which Grant gave as he pushed hard against the bow sent the motor-boat back into the river. Satisfied that there was nothing more to be done Grant once more turned and as fast as he was able ran toward the cottage located fifty yards back from the shore.

In response to his appeal two women and a man at once ran toward the place where Grant had left the girl.

"Please look after her," said Grant hastily. "I want to go back to help the others. We had an accident," he explained.

The boy was rapidly recovering his breath by this time and as already he had seen a little skiff at the nearby dock, without asking permission or explaining what he was about to do he ran to the place, cast off and leaped on board. A few powerful strokes sent him out upon the river once more and in a brief time he was near the place where the canoe was drifting.

Cautiously approaching it, he soon was able to grasp Miss Susie Stevens under her arms and draw her on board the skiff.

By this time the motor-boat had approached the spot, but Grant called to Fred, "I'll take her right ashore where I took the other girl. Wait for me out here or at the dock."

"We'll help you," called George from the canoe.

"All right," answered Grant.

Nothing more was said while the skiff and the canoe were soon swiftly towed toward the dock.

Willing hands were there awaiting their coming, for the entire household now had been aroused and was watching the events on the river.

In a brief time Miss Susie was lifted to the dock. She was still able to stand and declared sturdily that she did not require any help. However, two of the women, one on each side, were helping her, and in a brief time she was assisted to the house and taken within the cottage.

"What shall we do now, fellows?" inquired Grant blankly as he turned to greet his companions.

"We had better wait," replied George, "and take them back home as soon as they are able to go."

"I guess that's good advice," responded Grant.

Shouting to Fred he bade him bring the Black Growler to the dock and make her fast there while they waited for the more complete restoration of the girls whom they had rescued.

CHAPTER XVII

SENDING FOR SAM

The waiting of the boys continued longer than any of them had expected.

An hour passed and still no one appeared from the cottage.

"I wonder if there's anything wrong," said Fred as he glanced anxiously at the door.

"I guess not," answered George promptly. "The girls probably are exhausted, but I don't think there's anything serious. They came out of it a good deal better than I was afraid they would at first."

Following George's statement, the two girls were seen at that moment departing from the house. Accompanying them on their way to the dock were several members of the household who were doing their utmost to assist them.

Apparently, however, their services were neither required nor requested, for in a moment both girls moved quickly in advance of the little company and approached the dock.

Stepping quickly on board, Miss Susie said, "What did you do with my canoe?"

"We have got it here for you in tow. We thought you would probably want to take it with you and we're going to carry you home."

"That's very good of you," laughed the girl as she glanced back at her companion to make sure that she too had boarded the motor-boat.

"If you're all ready to go," suggested Fred, "we'll start right away. We have been waiting until you were ready."

"That's very good of you," again said the girl quickly. "I haven't thanked my life preservers yet for what they did. If you had not been there where you were the accident never would have happened," she added boldly.

For a moment the four Go Ahead boys stared blankly at the girl, who apparently had forgotten all their efforts to rescue her and her companion. Fortunately for the boys they had had other suits of clothing in the cabin of their boat so that all four now were clothed and dry. But to have all their heroism forgotten and to be blamed for being the cause of the accident was something which had not even remotely occurred to them.

"Yes," declared the girl, "if you had left us alone we wouldn't have tipped over."

"What was it we did?" demanded George.

"Why you came up with your old motor-boat and when I tried to be polite, Mildred thought she had to do the same thing, and then over we went."

"Well, that was the time when it was fortunate for you that we happened to be nearby," said John dryly.

"That's just what you had to do; you couldn't have helped yourselves."

In spite of the words of the animated girl, who apparently now had recovered her spirits and strength, it was plain to the boys that she was genuinely grateful for the rescue which they had made. She was a deeply interested spectator of the work of the boys in casting off and starting their swift boat and even insisted upon being permitted to steer part of the way.

"Have you joined the yacht club yet?" she inquired.

"What's that?" demanded George.

"Why the St. Lawrence Yacht Club. I am sure Fred's grandfather must belong and probably that will be enough of an introduction. We have some fine times there. Tennis all day, dances in the evenings and I don't know what all. You must be sure to come over there."

"You may be sure we'll come," spoke up George promptly. "Now I want to know," he added, "what our reward is to be for our heroic rescue of two forlorn maidens who were sinking in the cold waters of the St. Lawrence River."

"I think virtue will have to be its own reward in this case," laughed Mildred. "You ought to be satisfied with the honor you have won."

Fortunately the island which Mr. Stevens had rented was not far distant and not many minutes had elapsed before it was plainly seen by them all.

Before a landing was made, however, Miss Susie Stevens had suggested numerous plans for picnics, cruises among the islands, meetings for tennis at the yacht club and various other methods by which the days were to be passed.

As soon as their passengers departed, the Black Growler was headed swiftly for Chestnut Island, the name by which the place owned by Fred's grandfather was commonly called.

Upon their arrival they were informed that already Mr. Button had telephoned for Sam Hodge and that he had received word that the man would arrive the following morning.

"I hope he'll bring all his legs, and arms with him," suggested George with a laugh.

"What do you mean?" inquired Mr. Button.

"Why, he has a choice assortment," explained George. "It seems he used to work in a shop on Broome Street in New York City where they make legs and heads and arms for dummies."

"I don't understand yet," said Mr. Button blankly.

"Why, these wax figures that they have in the windows," explained Fred. "It was in a place where they make them that Sam Hodge worked and he made us all laugh when we took him on at Henderson Harbor. He was telling us about the boss throwing his leg at him and Sam told us he fired a foot back and before he had gone very far we had the air full of eyes, heads and legs and arms, feet and hands and everything else that goes to the making of a dummy. In fact I have almost come to believe that Sam is pretty well made up himself. When he comes down to-morrow I'm going to ask him to let me take out his eyes, take off his hair, pull out a foot and an arm, and when he gets through I'll see just how much there is of the real Sam anyway."

The boys laughed as Fred pictured the condition in which the loquacious Sam would be left.

Their interest, however, was still great in the exciting events through which they recently had passed. Mr. Button was an interested listener and when the story had been all told he said quietly, "Mr. Stevens has been down here several summers. I have been afraid of that girl every year. If she doesn't find herself in the bottom of the river some time soon, I don't believe the fault will be hers."

"Why, what's the matter with her?" inquired Fred.

"She's too much of a tomboy."

"What's that?" inquired Grant, winking at the other boys as he spoke.

"Why, she does most of the things that the boys do. She plays tennis, shoots a rifle, paddles a canoe and manages the Stevens family."

"And that is why you call her a tomboy?" inquired Fred.

"Yes, sir, it is," said the old gentleman solemnly. "Girls didn't act that way when I was young."

"How did they act?"

"Why, they were taught to be ladylike."

"And what is ladylike?" asked Fred.

"Why, it is to act like a lady."

"Yes," protested Fred, "but why shouldn't a lady do these things you're speaking of?"

"Because they are not ladylike," replied Mr. Button testily.

"But why aren't they?" persisted Fred. "I don't see."

"That's because you haven't learned any sense yet," said his grandfather, irritated at last by the failure of his grandson to agree to all that he had said.

Fred laughed goodnaturedly, for behind the manner of his grandfather he knew there was a heart that was big and generous. Mr. Button occasionally stormed about the "present generation" being so markedly different and deficient in all the good qualities that marked the young people of his own younger days.

"What about that bond?" inquired John. "Have you heard anything more about it?"

"Not a word," said Mr. Button sharply.

Before the old gentleman turned away, however, for Fred suspected that the subject was not a welcome topic of conversation, he said quickly, "Where's the man that wanted the bond?"

"How should I know?" retorted his grandfather.

"Has he been back here?"

"No, sir, he hasn't."

"Do you know where he is?"

"I'm not sure if I did that I should tell you."

"But you said he went to Syracuse."

"If I did that's probably where he went."

"Yes," said Fred, still persisting in asking questions, "but you don't say whether he is coming back or not."

"That's quite true."

"Is he coming?"

"I cannot tell you."

"Don't you know?"

"Did any one ever hear such a pestiferous child!" said Mr. Button, laughing as he spoke. "His questions and his tongue run like a mill-tail."

"What's a mill-tail?" inquired Fred.

"There he goes again!" said Mr. Button, holding up both hands in mock despair.

"But I want to know whether or not you have been up to Cape Vincent to do anything about that bond," demanded Fred.

"The bond isn't registered in my name anyway," answered Mr. Button. "Probably I couldn't get it if I wanted to."

"But you don't answer my question."

"Go into the house now and get ready for dinner. If you haven't any plans made for to-morrow I may ask you to take me up to Cape Vincent in the Black Growler."

"Of course we'll take you," said Fred. "We should like nothing better."

"Then it's understood that to-morrow we'll go to Cape Vincent."

"But, Grandfather," said Fred before he went upstairs, "Susie Stevens and Mildred think they will want to go with us to-morrow."

"And you told them they might?"

"Yes, sir."

"Well, I don't see then but what you'll have to keep your promise, though you mark my words, young man, you'll be sorry you took that tomboy along with you. She'll get you into trouble just as sure as the sun rises. You mark my words."

Fred laughed and as he went to his room he had no thought how nearly his grandfather's words were to be fulfilled the following day.

CHAPTER XVIII

A TEST

Early the following morning when the Go Ahead boys went down to the dock, they found that Sam Hodge already had arrived and was busily at work on the Black Growler.

"Good morning, Sam," called Fred, deeply interested in the sight of the investigation which Sam was making.

"'Mornin'," called Sam, without looking up from his task.

"How do you find everything on the boat?"

"I haven't only seen a few things yet," retorted Sam. "I'll tell you later what I think about it."

"Did you bring along any extra legs or arms?" asked George.

"Nothin' much," replied Sam. His manner, however, to the boys seemed to imply that he was holding some information in reserve and this fact at once increased their curiosity.

"What have you got?" asked George.

"I have nothin' much, but an albuminoid rib."

"What kind of a rib?"

"That's what you call it. If it isn't that it's alkali."

"What kind of a rib is an alkali rib?" asked John.

"Why, it's one of those things that's about as light as paper. Here, I'll show it to you," he added as he drew from his inner pocket a metal rib, which he at once handed to Fred.

"That looks like aluminum to me," said Fred quickly.

"That's just what I said," retorted Sam. "I thought I'd bring it along in case anything happened. I'll have some feet and hands comin' later."

"What for?" laughed Fred.

"What do you s'pose they're for? They're for you to wear."

"If you had brought along a head," said Grant solemnly, "it might have been a good thing. I have known Fred to lose his several times."

"We don't furnish brains, we just use them," said Sam as he restored the rib to his pocket. "Now, then," he added, "I'm goin' to give this here boat an overhaulin' from stem to stern."

"There isn't anything wrong, is there?" inquired

Fred anxiously.

"I told you I can't say yet," answered Sam. "I don't know until I have investigated. Can't expect much when a lot of harem scarem boys are driving such a machine as this is. Had any more trouble since I left you?"

"We haven't had any," answered Fred. "We helped pull a couple of girls out of the river yesterday."

"What was they doing in the river?" demanded Sam, looking up for the first time since the arrival of the boys.

"What most people usually do when they can't swim," answered Fred.

"What was the trouble?" asked Sam.

"The chief trouble was," said Grant solemnly, "that they did not have any alkali heads. Their heads were made of bone and were solid all the way through."

"The worst of it is," broke in Fred, "that they said we were to blame for spilling them into the river."

"Maybe you were," said Sam. "One never knows. Maybe they saw you trying to steer this boat."

"That's it. That's it exactly," spoke up George quickly. "I hadn't thought before why those girls were spilled out of the canoe. I don't wonder they wanted to drown themselves when they saw the way Fred steered."

"That's all right," retorted Fred as his friends all

laughed. "We'll take the Growler out this morning and see how she behaves. That's what Sam wants to do, I know. He can't tell how she runs until he sees her in action. Besides, my grandfather wants to go up to Cape Vincent and we promised to take those girls along."

"Better not," said Sam quickly. "I should think you had had experience enough. Don't you know that every sailor says that it is bad luck to bring a woman aboard ship?"

"The girls weren't on board. If they had been there wouldn't have been any trouble," asserted Fred.

"Well, go up and get your breakfast," said Sam, "and by the time you're ready, I guess we'll start."

The Black Growler stopped at the dock of the Stevens' and after waiting a half-hour Miss Susie and her friend appeared and took their seats on board the motor-boat.

Mr. Button was not enthusiastic in his morning salutations, evidently sharing in Sam's superstition that ill luck might follow the reception of their visitors.

Apparently the boys were not alarmed, however, and in a brief time the Black Growler sped forward on her way, and the sounds of laughter that came from her occupants were not indicative that trouble of any kind was greatly feared.

"Grandfather," said Fred, "I would like to try the boat to-day over the course or at least over part of the course that we'll have to run in that race."

"Well, if you want to try it," broke in Sam, who was

steering the boat, "why don't you? There isn't anything to prevent you that I know."

"All right then, we will," said Fred. "We'll run up to Cape Vincent first and on our way back we'll try out the course a little. Maybe we'll try only one leg of it -"

"Only one what?" broke in Sam, abruptly looking back at the boys as he spoke.

"Oh, it's not an albuminoid rib, Sam, it's just one leg of the course. They don't have any artificial legs in such places."

"You never can tell what will happen," said Sam; "you'd better bring one along."

"Why don't we try out the leg that we'll have to follow when we go up the river anyway?" inquired John. "Part of the course will be up stream and we might as well try that out now as any time."

"Is she in shape for trying it?" inquired Mr. Button of Sam.

"I haven't tried yet," said Sam cautiously.

"Then you never will know until you try," laughed Mr. Button. "When we strike the beginning let her go for a little while anyway, and we'll see how she works out."

In a brief time the swiftly moving Black Growler arrived near the spot which Fred had been informed would form one of the points in the triangular course over which the race was to take place.

"I guess you have got some friends that want to try out the course too," suggested Sam, pointing as he spoke to a motor-boat apparently of the same size as the Black Growler.

Instantly glancing in the direction indicated by Sam, the Go Ahead boys discovered the Varmint II nearby and from her actions it was plain that she too was planning to test the course.

"Make her show what she can do!" said George eagerly, a demand in which Miss Susie quickly joined.

"That's right," she exclaimed. "I just love to go fast. You can't make the Black Growler move too fast to suit me."

The two boats now were following parallel lines, although they were more than one hundred feet apart. It was manifest also that the crew of the rival boat were aware of the purpose in the minds of the Go Ahead boys and that they also were not unwilling to discover what one of their rivals might be able to do in the coming race.

Conversation ceased as suddenly the Black Growler darted forward almost as if she was a thing alive. The Varmint II started at the same moment and an impromptu race was on.

The bow of the Black Growler at times seemed almost to be lifted above the river. Dashes of water when the bow again struck were driven into the faces of all on board. The spray soon made the cockpit as wet as if a stream of water had been played upon it. The noise of the engine, the splash of the water, the rushing river, the white and excited faces, as well as the anxiety with which the Go Ahead boys watched the speed of their rival, all combined to increase the prevailing excitement. Apparently the two boats were moving almost neck and neck.

"We don't seem to gain on her, Sam," shouted Fred.

Sam turned and glared upon the boy, but did not reply to the suggestion. He was giving his entire attention to the task of steering the boat, glancing occasionally at his rival, which tenaciously was holding to its course.

Several steamboats were passed and as the sight of the racing boats was seen there was a wild rush of the passengers to the rail to watch the contest.

For twenty minutes the unexpected race continued. At the expiration of that time the Varmint II changed her course. Veering to the left she swerved in a wide semi-circle, saluting the Black Growler several times as she turned her course backward.

"I guess that will be some race," said Miss Susie Stevens. "I think I'll go with you."

"You think you'll what?" demanded Mr. Button sharply.

"I just said that I thought I would be one of the crew of the Black Growler in the race."

"Excuse me, young lady," said Mr. Button solemnly. "That will be no place for a lady."

"Why not?" demanded Miss Susie unabashed.

"All you have to do is to look at yourself now," retorted Mr. Button somewhat tartly. "You're soaked, you're dripping from your head to your heels."

"I don't mind a little thing like that."

"Well, you ought to, whether you do or not. When I was your age the girls didn't go in for racing."

"Then they never knew what they lost."

"No, they didn't know what they lost," said Mr. Button quietly. "I guess they were better, if they were not better off."

"Oh, you'll enjoy having me about, Mr. Button," said Miss Susie. "You need all the help you can get and Fred says he's going to steer in the race. He'll want me close by to tell him just what to do."

"If you speak to mo while I'm steering the boat in that race," spoke up Fred, "I'm afraid you'll find yourself where you and Mildred were yesterday when the Black Growler came along."

The fearless girl laughed derisively, but as the impromptu contest now was ended, conversation turned to other topics.

The speed under which the Black Growler was moving was somewhat diminished, but the motor-boat still was sweeping swiftly on its course.

"I hope we'll get there in time for luncheon," exclaimed Miss Susie at last breaking in upon the silence that had followed her conversation with

Fred's grandfather.

"That's another thing," said Mr. Button, "that I don't approve."

"What's that?" inquired Miss Susie. "Luncheon? Doesn't it make you hungry to ride on the river?"

"When I was young," said Mr. Button, "the girls didn't gorge themselves, and many a time I have seen my sisters even at a formal dinner eat only enough to enable them to follow the courses."

"Yes, and afterwards," said Miss Susie, who was unterrified by the gloomy remarks of the old gentleman, "they used to go behind the pantry doors and eat pickles and lots of other indigestible things. I don't wonder that they had such frightful color."

"But they didn't have such 'frightful color,' as you are pleased to call it," said Mr. Button. "When they were exposed to the sunlight they wore veils and protected themselves."

"And afterwards," said the girl, "they died of consumption. Now, honestly, Mr. Button, didn't some of these girls that you're speaking about die when they were young?"

"Death is no respector of persons. He cuts down the young as well as the old."

"Do you mean that for an answer to my question?"

The conversation which was becoming slightly heated abruptly ceased when George excitedly called the attention of his companions to a man standing on the dock in Cape Vincent which they were rapidly approaching.

"There's your bond man," he said in a low voice.

Instantly the eyes of all were turned toward the individual to whom George had referred. One look was sufficient to convince all the Go Ahead boys that George had spoken truly, and that the man before them was indeed the one who had demanded that the bond which the boys had discovered on board should be given to him.

CHAPTER XIX

THE LOST FISH

"You come with me, Freddie," said Mr. Button. Fred's face flushed at the term applied to him by his grandfather and still deeper color appeared in his cheeks when he saw a mischievous expression appear in the eyes of the girls. To be called by the name be which he was called when he was a little fellow, or at least very much smaller than he was at the present time, was the last thing that could be applied him in the way of teasing. Mr. Button, however, had no thought of annoying his grandson and used the term simply because it had been familiar to him from the time when Fred was born.

"Good-by, Freddie, good-by," called the three Go Ahead boys together, as their comrade obediently followed the call and at once joined his grandfather and the man who had demanded the bond and turned into the street.

"That fellow was waiting for us," exclaimed George in surprise. "I believe that Mr. Button knew all the time that he was to be here."

"Well, what do you make of it?" inquired Grant.

"I don't know what to make of it. That man and a lot of his friends from the canal-boats force their way on board the Black Growler and leave only when they are scared by the coming of the Caledonia. Then the first thing we know he shows up here at Cape Vincent and orders us to give up a bond which he says we have."

"And the worst of it is that we have it," said George ruefully.

"Had it, you mean," suggested Grant soberly.

"That's right," joined in John. "We gave it up and had it recorded in Fred's name. Now I suspect that those two men somehow have put up a job on Fred and that we'll lose our bond."

"'Our' bond is good," scoffed George.

"Well, whose is it?" demanded John.

"That's what we don't know, but that doesn't mean that everything we see, which may be the property of somebody we don't know, belongs to us."

"Well, if this Mr. Somebody owns that bond why doesn't he come and claim it?" retorted John.

"It's my opinion that Mr. Somebody has come," said Grant dryly.

"What do you mean?" inquired George.

"I don't know that I mean anything. I'm thinking though that the man who owns that bond, if it is good for anything, isn't going to rest easily until he finds out where it is."

"Do you think that boatman owns it?" asked John.

"It's plain that he knows something about it," answered Grant.

Meanwhile the two girls in the party were becoming somewhat impatient.

"My, nobody knows how thirsty I am!" said Miss Susie, who had been an interested listener and for some strange reason had not joined in the conversation.

"Plenty of water around here," suggested John.

"I don't mean that," said the girl quickly. "I mean something cold."

"And frozen?" asked John.

"My, how quick witted you are!" laughed the girl. "That's exactly what we want."

"I suppose we might as well give in first as last," said George in mock despair. "If anybody knows where we can get any ice cream we'll start."

"We'll start anyway," spoke up Miss Susie. "If we start we shall find it."

Evidently success attended the efforts to locate the ice cream parlors for long before the return of the boys and girls to the Black Growler, Fred and his grandfather had come back, the latter becoming more impatient with the failure of the young people to appear.

Sam Hodge meanwhile had been busily engaged in his inspection of the machinery of the Black Growler. When his task was completed he did not make any remarks, but his face apparently beamed with satisfaction.

"Sam," said Fred, "what do you think our chances are against that Varmint II?"

"'Gainst the which?" demanded Sam.

"That motor-boat that we were racing."

"I think it will depend somewhat on how fast we go," said Sam.

"What a wise man you are," laughed Fred. "I might have thought of that myself if I had tried hard. Do you think we can beat that boat? That's what I want to know."

"I think we can if we go faster than she does," replied Sam.

"Well, can we make her go faster?"

"You can if the speed is in her."

"Well, do you think the speed is in her?"

"I can't say just yet," said Sam, who was not to be moved from his cautious position. "Here come your friends," he added as the boys and girls were seen approaching the dock.

Mr. Button grumbled over the delay which had been

caused by the failure of the young people to return, but as no one except Fred understood just what he was saying slight attention was paid him.

Meanwhile at Sam's command the engine was started, and the Black Growler, free from the dock once more, soon was noisily and speedily making her way down the mighty river.

"Why didn't you beat that other boat?" demanded Miss Susie of Fred.

"That wasn't what we were trying to do."

"Well, what were you trying to do?" demanded the girl.

"Testing our boat and at the same time trying to find out what time they could make in the Varmint II."

"Well, did you find out?"

"We found that she can go," answered Fred somewhat dolefully. "Sam here says that we can beat her if we can go faster than she does."

"That's exactly what I say," spoke up Sam.

"How many legs have you got, Sam?" asked George abruptly.

"Six," answered Sam.

Both girls looked up in surprise. Miss Susie said, "He's a regular centipede. What does he mean?"

"What do you mean, Sam?" said Fred. "Miss Susie doesn't understand you. How many legs really have you got?"

"I have told you once," retorted Sam. "I have got six here and about fifty in New York."

The girls stared blankly at each other and then as the boys laughed, Miss Susie said, "What's the joke?"

"No joke," said Fred. "It's just a fact."

The attention of the party, however, was speedily attracted by the sight of a little boat that was approaching, flying a white flag at the stern.

"Oh, I know what that is," said Miss Susie confidently. "That means that somebody is sick on board and that they are signaling us to help them."

"Huh!" grunted Mr. Button.

"That's not it," responded George.

"Well, what is it then?" demanded the girl.

"It means that somebody on board has caught a muscallonge and they are bringing it in. If any boat catches one it usually puts straight for home and it isn't backward in letting the world know what has happened."

"Have they got the fish with them?"

"Why don't you ask them?" laughed George, handing the girl a megaphone as he spoke.

Quickly taking her place on the deck, Miss Susie shouted, "Have you got a muscallonge?"

"Yes," replied somebody on board.

"Hold it up and let us see it."

In response a man on the other boat held forth to view a huge fish which weighed at least twenty-five pounds."

"Good for you! Good for you!" shouted the Go Ahead boys together.

"Hold it up higher," called Miss Susie. "Is that a real fish? Did you really catch it or did you buy it somewhere?"

A reply was not given the questions, for suddenly the great fish slipped from the hands of the man who was holding it and with a splash it fell into the water.

"That's right," grunted Mr. Button. "I told you what was going to happen."

"Why, Mr. Button," exclaimed Miss Susie, "did you know beforehand that he was going to drop that fish?"

"I told the boys before we started that they would surely have trouble to-day. Now, stop this boat, Sam Hodge," he added. "We have got to help those people get that fish in."

"I guess they won't need any help," said Sam, who was watching the efforts of the men on the other boat. Its speed had been checked as soon as the accident had occurred and the two men on board quickly began to pull in the two skiffs, which they had in tow.

In a brief time they took their places on board one of the little boats and with long strokes started swiftly back in their search for their lost prize.

Fortunately the men soon found the floating muscallonge which now had been dead two hours. Eagerly they drew the fish into their skiff and when they returned to their motor-boat they were aware for the first time that the Go Ahead boys were there to help.

Few remarks, however, were made and as soon as the muscallonge had been restored to its place both boats continued on their way.

"I'm afraid," muttered Mr. Button, "that isn't the last thing that is going to happen to-day."

"I hope not," said Miss Susie lightly.

Apparently all the efforts of Fred's grandfather to subdue the light-hearted girl were doomed to failure. Why his prejudice against her had become so strong it was difficult even for Fred to understand, although he was familiar with the peculiar ways of Mr. Button.

"Look yonder!" suddenly exclaimed John, "That's the Varmint II again."

Coming around the end of a nearby island the swift little motor-boat was seen approaching.

Taking his megaphone Fred shouted, "Come on, we'll try it again! We couldn't do much this morning."

"All right," came back the answering hail from the Varmint II and in a brief time both boats were swiftly moving down the river.

Again the spray dashed over each party, the water through which they were passing again seemed to be moved as if by some intense heat beneath it. The noise of the motor and the sound of the rushing water made it difficult for the Go Ahead boys to hear one another.

There was slight disposition however, to talk, for all on board the little boat were eagerly watching their rival. Although there were no sure grounds for their belief, the Go Ahead boys were confident that the strongest rival they would face in the coming race was the boat which now was only a few yards distant.

And what a beautiful little structure she was. Her lines were all graceful and as she slipped through the water she seemed almost to share in the prevailing excitement.

Steadily the two boats continued on their way, neither apparently being able to gain much upon its rival. Occasionally the Varmint II led by a few feet, only to lose the advantage as the Black Growler slowly drew ahead. Evidently they were evenly matched. This fact, however, served only to increase the interest of the Go Ahead boys.

When at last the Varmint II again turned from the course and with a wide sweep started across the river there had been no sure test of the comparative speed of the two boats.

"What do you think, Sam?" inquired Fred anxiously. "Can we beat her?"

"We can if we go faster than she does," replied Sam briefly.

CHAPTER XX

SAM'S WARNING

The thought of the race which was to take place within a few days and in which both the Black Growler and the Varmint II were to be contestants was in the mind of every one. In spite of the unwillingness of Sam to express his opinion as to the outcome, Fred insisted repeatedly upon asking what he thought. Again and again Sam evaded a direct reply as in one form or another he explained that all he did know was that the Black Growler would win if she could run more swiftly than the Varmint II.

As to the possibility of developing the required speed he was non-committal.

Conversation did not lag on the voyage down the river. The presence of Mr. Button as well as the fact that Fred apparently was somewhat reserved and uncommunicative concerning his recent experiences in Cape Vincent, caused the Go Ahead boys to neglect the topic of conversation which just then was uppermost in their thoughts. Time did not drag, however, and it was a merry party on the motor-boat which attracted the attention of many of the parties they met. In the most informal manner salutes were given and whistles were tooted whenever boats large or small passed.

In spite of Miss Susie's apparent carelessness she had provided a most excellent luncheon, to which ample justice had been done by all on board, including Mr. Button.

It was late in the afternoon, however, when the two girls were left at their cottage and the Black Growler sped forward toward Chestnut Island.

As soon as a landing was made Mr. Button at once started for the cottage.

Left to themselves Fred's three friends quickly turned upon him and eagerly began to question him concerning his experiences at Cape Vincent.

"Where's your man that wanted the bond?" demanded George.

"Did you get the bond?" asked Grant.

"Did you find out who that fellow is?" inquired John.

"Hold on, fellows," laughed Fred. "I'll take you one at a time, but I don't want you all together. Now then speak up, one of you. What is it you want to know?"

"Did you find out who that man is?" asked John.

"I fancy you're referring to the gentleman who requested us to deliver to him that five thousand dollar bond?" answered Fred.

"You catch my meaning exactly," answered John solemnly.

"Well, then, let me say that he is just as big a mystery to me as he is to you."

"Did he get the bond?" demanded Grant.

"I don't know."

"Weren't you with him?"

"I was, but not all the time."

"Did he go to the bank?"

"He certainly did."

"Weren't you there, too? Couldn't you see whether they gave him the bond or not?"

"Not being able to see through a foot wall, and a door still stronger, I am unable to give you the information you so courteously request."

"What do you mean? Can't you speak in plain English?"

"I'll do my best," laughed Fred, who so often had been the object of attention from his friends that now he was rejoiced that in a measure at least the tables were turned. "Well, we were at the bank," he continued. "My grandfather told me to stay outside while he went into Mr. Reese's office. They were in there about five minutes and then Mr. Reese came out and asked me to tell our canal-boat friend that his presence was desired in the office, so I went outside the bank and found the man they were looking for, gave him the message and then I went back."

"Didn't they want you in the office too?" inquired John.

"I didn't receive any strong urging to enter," laughed Fred, "so I decided it was better for me to stay outside."

"How long were they in there?" inquired Grant.

"I suppose it was about half an hour, but it seemed a good deal longer."

"Who came out first?"

"The canal-man."

"Was he alone?"

"Yes."

"How long before any one else came out?"

"Five minutes anyway, perhaps ten."

"What did your friend do?"

"He went out of the bank and that's the last I saw of him."

"You don't know then whether he went to the hotel or the station, or came down the river."

"I have told you just what I know and all I know. I can't do any more."

"So we're just as wise as we were when we began,"

laughed George. "We don't know what has become of our bond nor where the man that wanted it went. We don't even know whether or not it is in the bank yet."

"Don't begin on the list of things you don't know, George," said Fred soberly. "It'll take too much time."

"It's a good thing to know that you don't know. Some people that don't know, don't know that they don't know. Now, I know some things and among the things I know, I know that I don't know some things that I think I know."

The Go Ahead boys laughed as they all started toward the cottage to prepare for dinner.

The following morning Fred and George were the first to dress and together they made their way once more to the boat-house.

In a room above the slip, in which the graceful little motor-boat was resting, Sam Hodge was found. He had arisen two hours before this time and already had eaten his breakfast and was preparing for the duties of the coming day.

It was because of Sam's own choice that the room he occupied had been assigned him. And what a strange room it was. Sam had brought many of his own belongings among which were various pictures of the human anatomy, both external and internal. A life-size dummy stood in one corner of the room, the expression on its face being almost human in its dolefulness. In other parts of the room were legs, arms, feet and hands in various stages of completion. Sam explained that his love for the work which he did in the winter, when he was employed in the factory on Broome Street, New York, was present with him throughout the year.

"Yes, I like fooling around a boat in the summer time," he explained, "but you can't do that when the ice is about two feet thick. And yet if I go back to New York then I am all out of practice with my feet and legs and arms, so the only thing for me to do is to keep in the game. Besides, I like it and what a fellow likes to do isn't work, it's play. I'm finishing up that dummy," explained Sam to the boys when they entered. "One arm is a bit too long and one of the feet ought to have a number four shoe and the other about a number nine. I have seen people that way, but not very often."

"I should think you would wake up in the night with the nightmare," laughed George. "I think I should if I looked out and saw somebody over in the corner of the room still, staring and silent."

"Yes, some folks is easily scared," acknowledged Sam. "I've been over to Alexandria Bay," he added.

"When?" inquired Fred quickly.

"Oh, I guess I've been over two or three times. I've been asking some questions about those men that run the Varmint II."

"What did you find out about them?" inquired both boys eagerly.

"Accordin' to what I heard they aren't much good."

"What do you mean?"

"Why, I think they are a tough lot," said Sam, shaking his head. "The two fellows that own the boat are both of them sons of very rich men, who give them all the money they want to use. It hasn't done the youngsters any good, I guess, from what I heard. They bought the motor-boat expecting that there wouldn't be anything on the river that could touch her. They say they are pretty sore now that they have found that there is a boat which may give them a hard rub and perhaps take the cup away from them after all."

"Sam, if you win that race for us -" began Fred eagerly.

"I'm not going to win your race," broke in Sam. "I've heard you say that you're going to do the steering yourself and if you are, why the only thing I can do is to be a sort of court of appeals. I'll be there to help you out if something goes wrong. Now, we're up against a pretty serious proposition. Those fellows are bound to win that race and if they can't win it one way they are goin' to win it another."

"I don't see how they can win, Sam, if they don't go faster than we do."

"Maybe they can win," suggested Sam, "if we go slower than they do."

"That's the same thing," laughed George.

"Not by a jugful."

"Why isn't it?"

"Why, they may not be goin' so very fast and yet if our boat isn't in good shape it may be that they'll keep ahead of us and beat us."

"Well, that's just what you're here for," said Fred; "to see that nothing does happen to us or to our boat."

"Are you goin' to take them girls along that you had yesterday?" inquired Sam abruptly.

"Do you mean in the race?" asked Fred.

"What did you think I meant?"

"Well, we're not going to take them."

"Then maybe there'll be a chance to win out. I wouldn't promise anything with them on board, especially one of them. She's all right, but she would want to steer the boat and talk to the crew when it might be that the whole race was dependin' on what we were doin' right then and there."

"No, you can rest easy about that," said Fred. "There won't be anybody on board except the Go Ahead boys and you."

"Well, then," said Sam, "if that's the case then we'll have to keep a sharp watch on the Black Growler."

Sam's manner more than the words he spoke impressed the boys with the fact that he was holding back something that he had heard or knew concerning the possibilities of trouble for the swift little motor-boat. Just what they were, neither Fred nor George could conjecture. Their confidence in Sam was great and when they departed from the boat-house they made light of his fears.

"Sam is a regular old kill joy," laughed George.

"There has to be somebody," said Fred, "to take the joy out of life. It wouldn't be worth living if that wasn't so."

"Well, Sam does his best," said George with a laugh, "and the only reason why he doesn't succeed is because his bark is worse than his bite. We know he doesn't mean half he says."

"But why does he seem so worried about something happening to the Black Growler?"

"Oh, I don't know," said George. "That's just one of his notions, I guess."

It was not long, however, before both boys were excitedly aware that Sam's forebodings had been based upon a knowledge greater than that possessed by any of the Go Ahead boys.

CHAPTER XXI

THE SUMMONS IN THE NIGHT

On each of the three days that followed, the Black Growler was sent over a part of the course which had been mapped out for the race. The speed of the marvelous little motor-boat apparently was satisfactory to all concerned, except Sam. He growled and protested that there was something wrong with the boat and declared that unless they kept a careful watch, other things that would be still worse might occur.

On several occasions an impromptu race was had with the Varmint II. It was plain to the occupants of each boat that their rival was dangerous. Fred became more anxious with the passing days, sometimes being low spirited and declaring that there was no hope for the Black Growler.

He was easily routed out of his despondency, however, for it has been well said that it is not difficult for men to believe the things which they wish to believe.

"We'll be all right," said George confidently. "There wouldn't be any fun in a race if the other boat did not have some speed in her. But you just wait, Fred, and we'll show that Varmint II a clean pair of heels."

"I hope so," said Fred, his courage quickly rising again.

"By the way, Fred," said John, "you never told us any more about that man who came for the bond."

"I haven't any more to tell," said Fred quietly.

"Now look here, Peewee," spoke up Grant. "That bond wasn't yours. It belonged to the Go Ahead boys. I don't see why you assume all the rights of ownership."

"I don't," protested Fred. "The bond was registered in my name at the bank and so I had to go with my grandfather to see about it."

"Did that canal-man steal the bond?" asked John.

"I can't tell you," replied Fred.

"Do you mean you can't, or you won't tell?"

"A little of both," laughed Fred, eager to change the subject.

Throughout these conversations Sam Hodge seldom spoke. Indeed, as the time drew nearer the day of the race, his anxiety manifestly increased. He was busy on or about the boat throughout the day and even when night fell it was difficult to persuade him to retire to his room in the boat-house.

Once when Fred looked out of his bedroom window, in the moonlight night about twelve o'clock, he discovered Sam pacing back and forth on the dock. Just why he was so uneasy Fred did not understand and Sam did not offer any explanation.

On the following night not long after the boys had retired, they were awakened by a loud call from Sam Hodge.

"Hi! Hi there!" he shouted. "Come out here."

Hastily donning their clothing the boys ran out of the house and quickly joined Sam, who had leaped into a skiff that had been fastened to the dock and was now rowing swiftly toward the head of the island.

"What is it, Sam?" called Fred.

Sam, however, made no response and soon disappeared from sight around the bend in the shore.

"What do you suppose the trouble is?" inquired John.

"I'm telling you," said George, "that Sam has seen something that surprised him. He has been saying all the while that he was afraid something might happen to the Black Growler."

"But nothing can happen to her to-night. It's perfectly clear. There's no storm, and even Sam did not think it was worth while to run her into the boat-house."

"That may be just the trouble," suggested Grant.

"I don't know what you mean," retorted George, quickly turning upon his friend. "What might happen?"

"The thing that Sam seemed to be afraid of."

"But what is that?"

"Sam hasn't told me."

"That's all so," spoke up Fred, "but Sam has some reason for being worried. I don't know what it is, and I think he ought to tell us."

"Maybe he will when he comes back," suggested George.

"Back from where?" retorted John scornfully. "He's just started, and nobody knows where he is going or when he is coming back."

"He will be here within a few minutes," said Grant confidently.

True to Grant's suggestion, not many minutes had elapsed before Sam was seen approaching. He was rowing leisurely and apparently was neither alarmed nor excited.

As soon as he came within speaking distance, Fred called sharply, "What is it, Sam?"

"Did you see anything?" inquired Sam as he rested on his oars a few yards from the dock.

"Nothing, except you," answered Fred. "We saw you pulling as if your life depended upon it."

"It wasn't my life, exactly," said Sam slowly, "but there was a man here on the dock."

"A man?" exclaimed George. "Who was he? What was

he doing here?"

"That's exactly what I should like to know myself," said Sam shortly. "I was trying to find out and that was just the reason why I followed him."

"Didn't you see any one?" Fred asked.

"Yes, sir, I did," replied Sam.

"What was he doing?" inquired John.

"I saw a skiff headed for Alexandria Bay."

"How many were in it?"

"Two men."

"What were they doing?"

"The last I saw of them they were pulling as if for dear life. That was why I couldn't catch them."

"And you think they were here on our dock?"

"I do," explained Sam promptly. "I saw one man on the dock. Probably the other was in the skiff."

"What were they doing?"

"Nothing when I first saw them. They were just getting ready to do it."

"Do what?" demanded George.

"I guess it's time for you boys to go back to your beds,"

said Sam after a brief silence. "If you can't tell, then I'm not going to explain."

"Tell us, Sam, just what happened," pleaded Fred.

For a moment the man was silent and then as if thinking better of his resolution, he said, "The fact is, boys, there was some one in the boat-house. I was sure of it though I couldn't see any one. I heard him moving around and when I came out on the dock there I saw him just as plain as day. Just about that time he saw me too, and that was the first I knew that there were two of them, one in the skiff and one on the dock."

"Were they near the Black Growler?" inquired Fred, who was keenly aroused by the story Sam was telling.

"They couldn't have been nearer," declared Sam, "but when they saw me, they started out as if the evil one was after them."

"I don't wonder," suggested George.

"Huh?" said Sam quickly. "What's that you say?"

"I think it would scare anybody if he thought you were trying to catch him," said George glibly.

Mollified by the explanation, Sam continued, "They lighted out as soon as they both were in the skiff and the way they rowed was something marvelous. I chased them around the point, but if you'll believe me when I got there they were already more than half-way to Alexandria Bay."

"They must have traveled fast," laughed John.

"They didn't delay any, let me tell you," said Sam, shaking his head. "And they had good reason to hurry up."

"Was anything wrong with the boat?" asked Fred.

"I haven't found out yet. I don't think they had time to do much harm."

"What makes you think they wanted to harm the boat anyway?" asked Grant.

"Huh," said Sam, turning abruptly upon the speaker. "What else could they want here?"

"I don't know that they would want anything," said Grant quietly. "When you have made up your mind that somebody is trying to put the Black Growler out of business it is easy for you to believe that everything is working for that one thing."

"You don't know as much as you might," said Sam tartly.

"By which you mean?" inquired Grant.

"By which I mean just this," responded Sam warmly. "The people that own the Varmint II are a tough crowd. They are some young fellows that have got more money than they have sense."

"More dollars than cents, you mean, don't you?" interrupted George.

"That's what I said," retorted Sam. "They are betting all sorts of money on their boat. From what I heard over at the Bay they have staked more money than you would believe on their boat winning the race."

"Who told you about it?" inquired Fred.

"Never you mind that," said Sam. "I know and that's enough. Now, if they've got so much staked they wouldn't feel so very bad, would they, if anything happened to the Growler? It seems she's the only boat they are afraid of anyway, and if she isn't in the race why the Varmint II will just walk away with the cup."

"And do you really think," inquired Fred, "that they will try to damage our boat so that she can't be in the race?"

"I'm not saying they will," answered Sam, "but somebody might. Perhaps they wouldn't know anything about it."

"Do you think those men who were here to-night came to do that?"

"I'm suspicious," said Sam, "but I don't know yet how much damage they did. I called you because I thought I might need your help. There isn't anything more you can do now and you might as well go back to bed."

With the coming of the day most of the fears and anxieties of the boys departed. The alarm of Sam the preceding night appeared very differently now and they even were inclined to laugh at him for his fears. Sam, however, had fallen once more into one of his periods of silence and made no comment on the remarks of the Go Ahead boys.

"I'm going over to the Bay now," said Sam when the boys after breakfast approached the dock.

"Are you going in the motor-boat?" inquired Fred.

"Yes, sir."

"How long will you be there?"

"I don't know. Probably an hour."

"Then we'll go over with you," answered Fred. "Perhaps we'll find one of these fellows who were trying to blow up the Black Growler last night." "I'm not saying they were trying to blow her up," retorted Sam. "You don't have to blow up a boat to put it out of commission, do you? Her machinery is so fine that it wouldn't take very much damage to one part to throw the whole thing out of gear."

"That's true," said George, "but I don't believe, Sam, that there's need for our being scared. Probably those two men you saw last night were just stopping on their way back to the Bay from some of the islands."

Sam shook his head and although he did not speak, his action implied that the Go Ahead boys might soon be wiser than they were at that time.

Nor was his suspicion misplaced. Not many hours had elapsed before they were almost as strong as Sam in their belief that the Black Growler was not only an object of dislike, but also that there was a real peril that she might be so injured that it would be impossible for her to enter the race.

CHAPTER XXII

A COLLISION

In a brief time the Black Growler was fast to one of the side-docks and the party prepared to disembark.

"I'm not going to leave that boat without somebody stayin' on board," asserted Sam positively, when he was aware that the Go Ahead boys were all planning to accompany him.

"What are you afraid of?" inquired George. "There's some one around here all the time and no one could do any damage without being seen."

"It doesn't make any difference," asserted Sam. "A man might drop sand into the bearings or grease cups or do some other mean trick and nobody ever see him."

"All right, then," laughed George, "I'll be the goat. I'll stay here while you're gone. I guess I shan't be lonesome," he added with a laugh as he glanced at the increasing assembly which already had been drawn to the dock to gaze at the beautiful little motor-boat.

Soon after the departure of his friends, George seated himself in the stern of the boat and did his utmost to appear indifferent to the admiring glances and words of approval which now were coming from the spectators.

He had secured a copy of the morning paper and was pretending to be interested in the news he was reading.

Suddenly he partly dropped the paper as in the crowd he discovered the canal-man, who had demanded their bond at Cape Vincent. For some reason which George was unable to understand he did not advance to the boat, preferring to remain on the outskirts of the little assembly. The fact, however, that the man was there was in itself somewhat startling.

Still pretending to be interested in his paper, George did his utmost to follow the actions of the man whom he had discovered, but not many minutes had elapsed before he departed from the dock.

When his friends returned the strange man had not come back.

"Did anything happen?" inquired Fred eagerly as he stepped on board.

"What did you think was going to happen?" answered George somewhat evasively.

"I didn't think anything was," laughed Fred. "Sam is the only one who is worried."

"Well, he has some right to be worried, I guess," said George slowly.

"Why, what's wrong? What happened?" demanded Fred excitedly.

"Are you ready to explain what you did with that bond that belongs to the Go Ahead boys?" asked George slowly.

"No, sir, I'm not."

"Then you'll not be interested in the fact that the man who wanted it came down here to the dock while you were gone."

"He did? He did?" exclaimed Fred so eagerly that his friends all laughed. "What did he want?"

"That, sir, I can't explain to you at this time," answered George, striving to mimic the tones and manner of his friend. "It's difficult for me to tell the whole story unless I know what you all have to say."

"I have nothing to say," retorted Fred.

"Neither have I," responded George glibly.

Meanwhile Sam had cast off and with his boat-hook had pushed the Black Growler out into the stream. The graceful lines of the motor-boat were more distinctly seen now and the enthusiasm of the spectators was somewhat noisily expressed.

At that moment, however, the Varmint II came sweeping in a great semi-circle toward the dock and the attention of the assembly was quickly divided.

The boys were able to overhear the comparisons which were made, some of them favorable to one boat and some to the other.

The Go Ahead boys, however, were so deeply interested in the sight of their rival that they gave slight heed to the comments. They were keenly watching the young men on board, but in a few minutes they were beyond the sight of the dock and the Varmint II consequently no longer could be seen.

"I tell you, Sam is right," said George positively. "Those fellows on that Varmint II are a hard crowd. If they have been betting as much money as Sam says they have, it may be that there's some reason for his being afraid that some accident may happen to the Black Growler."

"It wouldn't do any harm to keep pretty close watch anyway," suggested Grant. "Whatever the weather is I think it will be better to run her into the boat-house every night and put double locks on the doors."

"We'll do more than that," said Sam. "We'll have somebody on the lookout. I guess it wouldn't be very much of a job for you boys to divide the night up into watches. I'll stay on duty until eleven or twelve o'clock and from then on until six wouldn't take more than an hour and a half from each of you."

"We'll do that," said Fred quickly. "That's a good suggestion, Sam."

"But if we have the Black Growler fast inside the boat-house how can any one get at her?" inquired John.

"My dear String," said Grant solemnly, "I fear now that the remark of that wise Englishman was correct when he said that Nature never built men seven stories high without the top lofts being left empty."

"I have heard you say that before," retorted John, irritated by the manner more than by the words of his friend.

"Well, all I can say is," said Grant, "if you have any gray matter up there where your brain ought to be located you had better begin pretty soon to make it work. If a man wanted to break into the boat-house he wouldn't have very much trouble in doing it, no matter how many padlocks we put on the doors."

"That's right," spoke up George. "He could dive under the doors, or smash in the window or cut out a glass and if there wasn't any one on guard he might never be detected. No, sir, we've got to establish a guard and the fellow who is on duty must keep up a regular patrol. He must keep walking around the dock all the time."

"And there may be some other ways by which they will try to get at us besides injuring our boat," suggested Grant.

"I don't see what," spoke up John quickly. "It's the one boat they are afraid of and if they can only put the Black Growler out of business they won't have anything to fear, as far as the outcome of the race is concerned. What could they do anyway?"

"Oh, I don't know," said Grant. "I can think of a dozen tricks they might play, any one of which might throw us out of the race."

Grant's words proved to be more prophetic than he had dreamed. That very afternoon after the boys had taken their daily run over a part of the triangular course where the great race was to be held, an event occurred which confirmed his statement and added strength to Sam's warning.

The Black Growler already had finished her course and under low speed was moving with the current on her way back to the island where she belonged.

Suddenly and without any warning whistle, a swift little boat dashed out from behind one of the small islands which the Black Growler chanced to be passing at the time and almost before the boys were aware of what was occurring there was a collision.

"Look out! Look out there!" shouted Fred, who was steering, in his loudest tones. At the same time he did his utmost to change the course of the motor-boat. His words of warning, however, were either unheard or unheeded. There was a sharp collision, for the smaller boat was moving swiftly. This was followed by the sound of a grinding crash. In dismay the Go Ahead boys ran to the side of their boat and speedily discovered that the metal bow of the little boat before them had cut a long gash which extended below the water's edge. Indeed, it was only by an effort that the other boat was freed. To all appearances she was uninjured. On board were two men, plainly belonging to the region.

"What's the matter with you?" called one of the men on the other boat.

"What's the matter with you?" retorted Fred. "Why didn't you whistle before you turned the end of the island?"

"How were we to know anything was there if you

didn't let us know? You, yourself, ought to have whistled."

The damage to the Black Growler, however, was not to be explained away by abuse or questions. Sam, already in the skiff, had brought it along-side and was inspecting the damage on the outside. As yet he had not made any suggestions and how serious the collision might prove to have been was not yet known.

Meanwhile the other boat hastily withdrew and when the Go Ahead boys again looked up to discover where it was, not one of them was able to find it.

"That's a great note!" exclaimed George in disgust. "They not merely ram us, but they don't wait nor even offer to help us."

"They didn't want to help," grumbled Sam. "The sooner they could get away from here, the better."

"What do you mean?" said Grant, abruptly turning to face Sam as he spoke.

"It seems to me," spoke up John, "that Nature doesn't have to make every fellow seven stories high to leave his topknot vacant. Sam thinks those fellows ran into us purposely."

For a moment the Go Ahead boys stared blankly at one another. The suggestion of John in the light of what had occurred after the accident might be true. The men in the other boat were strangers to the boys, not one of whom had ever seen either of them before.

The silent manner in which the sharp little boat had

come around the island also was suspicious. With redoubled anxiety the boys turned to Sam to discover how serious was the damage which had been inflicted.

"How do you find it, Sam?" called Fred anxiously. "Are we out of the race?"

Sam shook his head as if he either was unwilling or unable as yet to reply.

Meanwhile the Black Growler had been drifting with the current, all power instantly having been shut off. Slight effort was required to keep her headed aright and Fred had remained at the wheel when Sam had begun his investigations.

Conversation now ceased while all four boys anxiously awaited the results of Sam's efforts to discover whether or not the Black Growler had suffered serious damage.

CHAPTER XXIII

THE CALL IN THE NIGHT

The only announcement which Sam vouchsafed after he had completed his hasty inspection of the damage which had been done was, "I guess she'll stand it all right as far as Alexandria Bay."

"Are you going to drift all the way, Sam?" inquired John.

"Drift? No! I'm going ahead. Seems to me I've heard some boys talk about 'goin' ahead,' and now 's the time to find out whether they mean business or not."

Relieved by the manner of Sam, although he had not made any positive statement, the four Go Ahead boys eagerly watched him as under slow headway he carefully guided the swift little boat toward its destination.

An hour afterward, they arrived at Alexandria Bay. There Sam insisted once more upon the boys remaining on board while he sought the help he desired in repairing the Black Growler.

While the boys were awaiting his return, their conversation naturally turned upon the mishap which had befallen them and their anxiety concerning the outcome of the accident.

"I'm telling you," said John, "that I haven't seen but one fellow on the Varmint II that was on board when I came up the Hudson with them."

"What has become of the others?" inquired Fred.

"I don't know. I haven't seen any of them. I remember that one particular fellow because he made me think when I saw him that there weren't many things he would hesitate to do if he wanted to win pretty badly."

"Do you really think," inquired George, "that this 'accident' up here was not an accident at all? Do you honestly believe that they ran into us on purpose?"

"I'm not charging nobody with nothin', as Sam says," laughed John, "but it's strange that boat didn't give any warning."

"They said that we didn't give any warning either," spoke up Grant. "Perhaps we were as much to blame as they were."

"Well, if that's the only thing that happens to us," said Fred, "I shan't complain, that is, if the Black Growler isn't put out of the race."

"You'll have a good excuse, Peewee," laughed George, "if you lose the cup."

"How's that?" inquired Fred.

"Why, you can charge it up to the collision."

"I'm not going to charge it to anything but the boat," retorted Fred sharply. "If the Black Growler doesn't win it isn't going to be the fault of any one but herself. There comes Sam with two men," he added, as the boatman was seen approaching, accompanied by two mechanics.

Another inspection of the damaged boat was made by the men whom Sam had brought, but their verdict coincided with his own. The Black Growler was marred, but no serious damage had been done.

"You're sure there isn't any leak, are you?" inquired Fred anxiously after the work was completed.

"Not a leak," laughed one of the men.

"All the same," spoke up Sam, "I'm going to leave the boat here and I'll be back for her to-night. Don't let any one come near her, and give her a thorough overhauling."

The men readily consented and soon departed, taking the Black Growler around the point to the spot where their boathouse was located.

The Go Ahead boys and Sam then took their places in the two skiffs which the Black Growler had had in tow and in a brief time arrived at the dock on the island owned by Mr. Button.

Fred's grandfather chanced to be in the boat-house when they arrived and in response to his inquiry concerning the motor-boat, Fred briefly related the story of the accident.

"Who was steering?" demanded Mr. Button sharply. "That's what comes of letting a lot of boys run such a delicate piece of work as that motor-boat. I told your father, Fred, that he ought not to get you any such plaything as that. I'll warrant that you were steering and not paying any attention."

Fred laughed as he said, "The fact is, Grandfather, that I was on the lookout but the other boat never whistled nor gave us any sign of their coming."

"Did you let them know that you were coming?"

"Why, no, we didn't whistle."

"Then I don't see that you have any one to blame but yourselves," said Mr. Button tartly. "It's just as I said."

"But we're not so sure that it was an accident," persisted Fred.

"No," laughed Mr. Button. "I suppose you think that other boat was hiding behind the rock ready to jump out at you the way a pickerel starts for a minnow."

"If that was the only thing," explained Fred, "we might agree with you. But the trouble is that we're afraid somebody wants to injure the Black Growler."

"Why?" demanded Mr. Button, turning abruptly upon the boys as he spoke.

"To put her out of the race."

For a moment Mr. Button stared blankly at his grandson and then said quietly, "Don't you believe it.

We don't have that kind of people around here. I shall have to write your father that you were to blame."

"And I'll write him and tell him all about it," said Fred angrily.

"See that you do. See that you do," said his grandfather as he turned to the house and left the boys standing on the dock.

"All the same," spoke up George, "I'm sure that that collision wasn't any accident. What do you think, Grant?"

"I confess I don't know," replied Grant. "If it was the only thing that had happened I might think it was an accident, but taken in connection with some other things we have found out, I'm almost afraid it wasn't."

"Then the only thing for us to do," said John, "is to keep watch. Sam is going to bring the Black Growler back here to-night and some one of us will have to be on guard all the time."

"I have got that all fixed," said Fred, taking a slip of paper from his pocket as he spoke; "I have divided the night into five watches. We'll let Sam stay on guard until eleven o'clock. I'll take the watch from eleven P. M. to twelve-thirty A. M. Grant can come on at twelve-thirty and stay until two, then George will take his place and stay until half-past three. John will be the last one and he can be the guard from half-past three until five o 'clock. There won't be any need of any one after that because it will be light by that time."

"That's all right," spoke up George. "The only

suggestion I have to make is that we rotate the hours, if we keep this up many nights."

"What do you mean?" inquired Fred.

"Why the one that comes on at eleven o'clock one night comes on at twelve-thirty the next night. The one who comes on at twelve-thirty will report at two and so on. We'll just keep pushing the schedule up every night so we'll all be the same when we're done."

"How shall we know when our turns come?" inquired John.

"Every fellow is to call the one who is to take his place."

"But suppose the villain comes between spells?"

"We'll have to take our chances on that," said John.

The proposed scheme was finally accepted. About six o'clock Sam returned with the Black Growler and when the plan was explained to him he readily consented to accept the part which had been assigned to him.

That night at eleven o 'clock he called Fred who was to have the first watch. After the first half-hour the young guard in the silence that rested over the great river found the time dragging heavily. In order to keep awake he walked about the dock, peering intently in every direction. Not a sign of danger had been discovered, however, when at half-past twelve he summoned Grant to take his place.

Grant also was not molested and when he called George at two o'clock he said sleepily, "It all seems like fool business anyway, Pop."

"You've been asleep," retorted George.

"I haven't closed my eyes," retorted Grant sharply. "If you do as well you'll be lucky."

A half-hour after George had entered upon his task he stopped and peered through the window into the boathouse. The light of the moon made many of the objects within clear and distinct. The Black Growler was lying peacefully in her slip. Apparently peril was nowhere threatening.

Suddenly, as George glanced at the farther end of the platform beside the slip, he stopped abruptly and stepped quickly back from the window. Approaching the place again, he cautiously peered within and his first impressions were confirmed. He was able to see distinctly the figure of a man crouching in a corner of the room.

Instantly George's heart was thumping wildly and he was tempted to shout to the intruder. Hastily banishing the impulse he watched the man. The dim outline of his figure was distinctly seen. Perhaps the intruder had been startled by the discovery of the face at the window. At all events he remained motionless and not a sound was heard save the lapping of the little waves against the dock.

By this time George's fears had returned in full force. He decided quickly to summon the Go Ahead boys and not attempt alone to drive away the intruder. That the man's purpose in coming was evil he had no question. What other explanation was to be had for the presence of a strange man in the boat-house at three o'clock in the morning?

Running silently and swiftly to the house, George speedily summoned his friends, who were wide awake as soon as the report of his discovery of the man in the boat-house was heard.

"Shall I take a gun?" whispered Fred to his companion.

"No," said Grant sharply. "We don't want any gun."

"Well, some of us ought to have clubs or something," persisted Fred.

"I don't think we shall want anything," said Grant, "but if you're afraid, bring along two or three bats."

These weapons were secured and then silently the four Go Ahead boys departed from the house and stealthily approached the boat-house in which George had discovered the presence of the intruder.

CHAPTER XXIV

THE MAN IN THE BOAT-HOUSE

When the Go Ahead boys drew near the dock they separated, George and Grant moving to one side of the boat-house while John and Fred approached from the opposite side. There were two large doors in the front of the boat-house, both of which now were closed. The upper part of each, however, was of glass and was so made that the boys were able to stand on the dock and by leaning forward could peer into the building.

"He's there," whispered George excitedly, after he had looked within. Quickly withdrawing, Grant took his place and silently peered into the slip. At the same time John and Fred were making their investigations on the opposite side of the slip, although Fred was having his difficulties because he was not tall enough to enable him to look through the glass.

The man whom George had discovered apparently had not moved from the place in which he had first been seen. Perhaps he too was listening and was fearful of an attack.

Their excitement now greatly intensified, George beckoned for John and Fred to come to the place where he and Grant were standing on the dock.

"He's there," whispered Fred.

"I told you he was," whispered George in reply. "Now the question is how shall we get him?"

"How did he get in?" inquired Grant.

"I don't know," replied George, shaking his head. "There isn't any window open and the doors are locked."

"He must have dived under the door and come up that way," suggested John.

"This isn't any time to be discussing how he got there," remarked George. "The thing for us to do is to find out how we are going to get him out or get him. Let's go around to the window on the river side."

In response to the suggestion the boys stealthily crept along the dock and then one after another cautiously peered through the window. Not one of them stood in full view of the man within, for they were aware of the peril that might follow such an action.

"He's still there," whispered Fred, "and I don't believe he has moved once since we came back."

"He's scared," suggested John. "He doesn't know which way to turn."

The suggestion that the intruder might be alarmed was new to the Go Ahead boys and did much to revive their courage.

John and George each had secured a bat when they had

left the house. And now they were prepared to defend the motor-boat and themselves also if the need arose.

"Knock on the window," suggested Grant. "Let the fellow know we're here."

"He may get away," warned George, who still was the most excited of all.

"If he tries to, we'll get him then anyway," said Grant. "Go around and look on the other side of the boat-house," he directed Fred and John. "We'll wait here. I'll rap on the window and we'll see what he does."

Grant waited until sufficient time had elapsed to enable his friends to take their position in front of the entrance on the opposite side and then rapped lightly upon the window. No response was made to his summons.

"He couldn't hear you," whispered George. "You'll have to make more noise than that."

Again Grant rapped upon the glass, pounding on the window sash also in his efforts to arouse the attention of the man within.

All four boys now were keenly excited and all were eager to discover what the intruder would do, now that his presence had been discovered.

To their surprise the man did not respond to the summons. Even his position was unchanged and in the dim light the boys were unable to decide whether or not he had even glanced in the direction from which the hail had come.

"There's only one thing we can do," said George.

"What's that?" demanded Grant.

"Go around to the other side and tell Fred we've got to have the door unlocked. Then we'll make a rush on the fellow before he knows that we are after him."

The suggestion was quickly followed and soon the four boys were standing together in front of the side-door which opened upon the dock.

"Now, then," said Fred, who insisted upon retaining his key, "when I unlock the door all four of us must make a rush together."

"That's right," whispered George as he grasped more tightly the bat which he was holding in his hand.

"Let String and George go ahead. They are the best armed," said Grant.

For some reason Grant was less excited than his companions, a fact which escaped the attention of the boys at that time.

"All ready!" whispered Fred. Quickly turning the key he opened the door and together the four boys darted into the boat-house.

Although the moon was shining, the interior of the room was somewhat darker than it had been on the dock. The boys, however, were able to see clearly the man who was still standing near the Black Growler. Not even when they rushed upon him did he turn his face toward them.

In their eagerness to secure him all four did their utmost to leap upon him at the same time.

A most amazing result, however, followed their desperate attempt. Despite his efforts to save himself, Fred, who pluckily was in advance, was pushed over the edge of the slip and with a loud splash fell into the river. Before he could check himself John followed his example. A yell came from Fred when he arose to the surface because at that moment the intruder, whom they had discovered in the boat-house, also followed the example set by the boys.

Meanwhile George and Grant had broken into loud laughter. George was bowed and slapping his sides as he moved about the room. Grant was laughing almost as loudly as his companion, although he did not move from the place where he was standing.

"Give us a hand," called Fred. "I can't see the ladder."

"It's right in front of you," suggested George, advancing to the edge and looking down into the water which was only about four feet below him. "There it is. Follow the sound of my voice."

"I don't see what there is so funny about all this," sputtered Fred as he climbed to the floor.

"Funny!" exclaimed Grant. "It beats anything I ever experienced."

"What's the trouble?" demanded John, who now also had climbed out of the water. His elongated form only partly clothed, his garments dripping and clinging to his slim body, increased the weirdness of his appearance.

"I think the joke's on George more than even it is on Peewee and String," laughed Grant.

At this moment Sam, who had been asleep in his room appeared, rubbing his eyes and gazing in surprise at the boys. "What's wrong?" he demanded gruffly.

"Nothing," said George, beginning to laugh again.

"It seems to me you make lots of fuss when nothin' is the matter. What are you all down here for anyway?"

"Why, George got us down here to help him get a man who was in the boat-house."

"Huh, what's that you say?"

"Why, George discovered somebody in the boat-house and he routed us all out to help him get him."

"Did you get him?" inquired Sam.

"We got all there was to get," laughed Grant.

"What do you mean?" demanded Sam, looking around the room and for the first time suspecting what had taken place.

"Why, we mean that you had that wax figure of yours down here and we all thought it was a man."

"I don't blame you," said Sam solemnly. "That's one of the best wax dummies I ever made."

"But why did you leave it where you did?" inquired George.

"Why, I figured it out this way," said Sam slowly. "If a scarecrow will keep crows out of a cornfield, why couldn't I rig up something to scare off anybody that wanted to damage the Black Growler?"

"That's good sense," said Grant soberly.

"Of course it is sense," declared Sam. "I put the dummy down there so that if anybody looked into the boat-house he would see it and he would think somebody was on guard."

"That's right," said Fred. "We had two dummies on guard to-night. One inside the boat-house and one outside."

"That may be all true," spoke up George, "but there was only one of them that followed you into the river."

"You would feel better if you had," declared Fred. "Now, then, I don't see that there's anything more for us to do except to go back to bed."

"But where's my dummy?" demanded Sam.

"That's right," said Fred. "We never fished it out of the river. I guess you'll find it all right, Sam, somewhere in the slip."

In a brief time Sam's possession was rescued from its place of peril, but the boatman's lamentations were the last words the boys heard when they departed.

"Color's all washed out. It doesn't look more than half human," Sam was declaring as he stood in the moonlight examining the dummy which he had fashioned after his arrival at the boat-house. "Sam has an extra assortment of legs and arms in his room," exclaimed Grant, as the boys entered the house. "He seems possessed to have them around him."

"Perhaps they will come in handy some day," laughed George.

"I don't know how."

On the following morning, however, when the Black Growler was withdrawn from the slip and once more was sent over a part of the course there was a goodly supply of Sam's legs and arms on board. Just why he had insisted upon taking them, he did not explain. So human were the pieces in their appearance that a stranger might have been startled when he first saw the heap.

As usual the Varmint II was speedily trailing the Black Growler. Indeed it was not long before the two boats were moving side by side, only a few feet intervening.

The Go Ahead boys had been singing a song which has long been famous on the St. Lawrence,

"Saw my leg off,
Saw my leg off,
Saw my leg off,
Short!"

"That's what you'll have to do," called one of the men on board the Varmint II, "to lighten your load the day of the race."

"We won't wait until then," called back George. "We'll

see if we can't lighten up a bit right now."

As soon as he had spoken, taking one of the artificial legs from the pile he flung it far behind the swiftly moving motor-boat.

Instantly the men on the Varmint II rushed to the stern of their boat and in astonishment were all looking at the leg which now could be seen floating on the surface of the river.

CHAPTER XXV

THE OWNER OF THE BOND

A loud laugh arose from the people on board the Varmint II when the floating leg was more clearly seen.

Indeed the last sound that came to the ears of the Go Ahead boys from their rivals when the boat no longer was seen was a mocking echo of their song,

"Saw my leg off -
Short!"

A half-hour afterward the Go Ahead boys stopped at one of the largest islands and all four went ashore.

On their return to the dock they were followed by a very persistent Armenian who apparently was unshaken in his determination to sell certain articles he was peddling.

"I tell you," said Fred sharply, turning upon the dark-complexioned man, "we don't want any of your rugs or table cloths."

"Yees, kind sir, but just see these mooch fine han'ki'chiefs."

"But we don't want any," said Fred.

"But, my gud sir, they are ver' cheep."

By this time the boys had arrived at the landing and still the persistent peddler gave them no rest. He was calling his wares and insisting upon an inspection of them, ignoring the protests of the boys.

Finally in despair Fred reached beneath the seat and drew forth one of Sam's artificial legs. He waved it before the startled Armenian who gazed at it a moment in manifest fear and then uttering a loud scream ran back to his basket.

A laugh arose from the assembly on the dock who had been watching the experiences of the boys. The Armenian, however, did not delay and when the Black Growler departed, the boys were able to see the disappearing figure of their tormentor walking rapidly up the hill.

There he turned and looked back at the dock, but although the boat had departed, apparently his fears were only slightly relieved, for he soon disappeared.

"That's the best thing we've found in a long while," laughed George. "The way for us to get rid of all peddlers is to shake an arm or wave a leg at them."

"We may have to try again before long," suggested Fred. "This is the time when most of the peddlers come here."

Meanwhile the Black Growler was moving swiftly down the river

The talk of the excited boys soon turned toward the prospect of the race and somehow it was manifest that a measure of confidence had returned to Fred. So much had been said of late concerning the prowess of the Varmint II by the boys who delighted in teasing their friend, that Fred had arrived at a stage of mind when it was difficult for him to distinguish between the words that were spoken in bantering and in earnest.

"I'll tell you what I'm going to do," said George as the swift little boat came within sight of Alexandria Bay.

"What are you going to do?" inquired John.

"I'm going to take my right arm out of my coat and tie it behind me. Then I'm going to put one of Sam's artificial arms in the sleeve and find somebody to shake hands with me. He'll shake so hard that I'm half afraid my arm will come off."

"That's all right," laughed his companions as they assisted George to carry out his plan.

When the motor-boat stopped at the dock the artificial arm had been placed in the coat sleeve and George was assisted to the dock.

There George discovered one of the men who had helped in repairing the Black Growler.

"Hello!" called the mechanic, discovering the boys and at once approaching.

"Hello, to you!" called back George. "It's been a long time since I have seen you. I shan't forget you for I have three or four good reasons."

"I hope you won't," laughed the mechanic, "but I should like to know what your reasons are."

"One reason," said George seriously, "was that you never shook hands with me in the morning when you came to work."

"I didn't know you wanted me to," said the man. "I'll make up for lost time now." As he spoke he grasped the hand which extended from George's right sleeve and as George at that same moment turned quickly away, the astonished handshaker stood holding in his grasp an arm which had apparently come from the sleeve of the boy.

"That's right," said George soberly, pretending to be much grieved. "That's right. First you don't shake hands and then you shake hands so hard that you take my arm right off."

The sight had quickly drawn many of the people who were loitering about the dock and for a moment they were startled to see what had been apparently a serious accident.

"It's nothing," said George, turning to the assembly. "This man shook hands with me and the first thing I know he had shaken my arm off. He's welcome to it, however, and I hope it will do him some good."

The crowd was laughing noisily by this time and when George turned back to resume his place on board the motor-boat, the mechanic was the center of an observing throng which was inspecting the arm that he still was holding.

Upon the return of the boys to the island, they discovered that Fred's grandfather was seated upon the piazza conversing with a man whose form impressed the Go Ahead boys as being familiar.

When they drew near the house John exclaimed in a low voice, "That's our friend that we saw on the canalboat."

His startled companions again glanced hastily at the man and Grant said, "You're right for once in your life, String. That's just who it is."

"What is he doing here?" demanded John.

"I can't tell you," said Fred.

"Was he expected this morning?"

"Not to my knowledge."

When the boys went up the steps, however, Mr. Button summoned all four to come to the place where he was seated.

Somewhat startled by the invitation the boys approached, all glancing in some confusion at the man seated near Mr. Button. He was dressed in a different suit now and many of his ways and manners had been changed for the better. He was now at his ease and the twinkle that appeared in his eyes was far different from the expression which the boys had seen there in their earlier experiences with the man.

"You appear to be acquainted with this man," suggested Mr. Button dryly.

"We have seen him before," said George.

"And not exactly where you wanted to see him, I fancy," laughed Mr. Button. "Do you know who he is?"

"No, sir," said George quickly, "and we don't know what he is either."

"Well, this is Mr. Brown from Syracuse," explained Mr. Button. "A gang of bank robbers got into one of the vaults there some time ago and got away with a large number of bonds. Mr. Brown was detailed to find and catch the thieves if possible."

As Mr. Button ceased speaking the interest and excitement of the boys at once increased.

They looked eagerly at one another and at Mr. Brown, who now assumed an importance in their eyes, which before he had not had, even when they believed him to be a false claimant to the bond which they had found on board the Black Growler.

"Are you a detective?" inquired John, turning to Mr. Brown as he spoke.

"I don't speak of myself in that way," replied Mr. Brown, "and yet -"

"That's what he is," interrupted Mr. Button "He already has run down and found most of the bonds."

"How did that one come to be on our boat?" inquired Grant.

"Why, I had it in my pocket," laughed Mr. Brown, "and I put it under the cushion for safe keeping. You see, I joined that crowd and they thought I was one of the canal-men. I was with them for ten days at least and finally I found out what I wanted to know."

"Were they the bank thieves?" asked George eagerly.

"Some of them," replied Mr. Brown. "They were strangely mixed up. In fact that is one of the tricks they have, I am told. When a bank is broken into if the men are successful they scatter so that no two are in the same locality. It took me a long time to get in with these men but I finally succeeded. Indeed the care of some of the stolen bonds was left to me. They were not very easily converted into cash by any of them and as they all believed I was really a yeggman they finally let me into their secrets."

"Where are they now?" asked Fred.

"Some of them are missing but two have been taken into custody. I have forwarded the bond, which you boys unconsciously were carrying on the Black Growler, to the bank to be restored to its proper owners."

After the boys went to their rooms they were still discussing the story of the lost bond.

The fact that one of the gang, which had forced its way on board the boat while they were passing through the Erie Canal, had turned out to be a detective, was sufficient to arouse the keenest interest among the Go Ahead boys. Indeed, in the afternoon they insisted upon Mr. Brown accompanying them once more while they made another test of the racing motor-boat on the course.

Mr. Brown, upon the insistence of the Go Ahead boys, related many of the stirring experiences which he had had as a detective and when he departed, after they had returned to the island, they were all delighted with the changed man. How he had been able to pass himself among the professional bank thieves as one of their number was an increasing marvel to all four.

It was still agreed that the boat-house must be guarded every night. The various watches were continued, for the fear of the boys that some evil might befall their boat was still with them.

Mr. Button laughed good-naturedly at their precautions, declaring that a thief was almost unknown in the entire region. However, he offered no objections and the boys arranged their vigils as on the preceding nights.

No evil had befallen the racing motor-boat, however when morning came.

The race now was only two days distant. Only one night therefore intervened and the irksome task of guarding the boat-house would only have to be performed once more. The vigil of the Go Ahead boys, however, was not rewarded by detecting the presence of any one with plots against the Black Growler.

The day of the race dawned clear and fair. The excitement among the boys had now become intense. Everything had been done for the swift little racer that had been in the power of the boys.

Her sides were glistening and her machinery oiled and polished and when at last she was declared by Sam to be ready for the supreme trial, all the Go Ahead boys were agreed that never before had their boat been more capable of making her highest speed than at the present time.

CHAPTER XXVI

CONCLUSION

When the Black Growler slowly moved forward to take her position in the line, the excited boys were aware that the shores of the nearby islands were filled with interested spectators. Outside the limits of the race there were scores of yachts and motor-boats, whose owners with their guests had assembled to watch the exciting contest. Patrol boats were noisily demanding that the line should be kept clear and were busily speeding back and forth to see that their demands were strictly enforced.

Before the boys had left Chestnut Island, Miss Susie Stevens and her friend had arrived, the impulsive girl begging that she might be permitted to be one of the company on board the Black Growler during the race.

Her request, however, was denied. Only the four Go Ahead boys and Sam were to be on board to manage the swift little craft.

When the boys advanced toward the starting place, they discovered, after lots had been drawn for positions, that they were next to the Varmint II, the latter boat having drawn number four, while its chief rival was fifth in the line.

"Those fellows aren't so bad, after all," said George good-naturedly to his companions when he saw the five men that were on board the rival boat. "There we were suspecting them of all sorts of tricks and yet nothing happened to the Black Growler. We had our troubles for our pains."

"Huh!" interrupted Sam. "You aren't out of the woods yet. There's no knowing what may happen before we turn the last stake."

"Sam," demanded Fred anxiously, "have you any reason to suspect anything more?"

"Nothin' except that I know those fellows will not stop at anything to win the race. They have a lot of money bet and they aren't goin' to lose it if they can help it."

"Well, I shan't have any sympathy for them if they do lose their money," spoke up Grant, "at least if they lose it by betting on their boat. I don't believe in that thing myself. I don't want any money that I haven't honestly earned."

"That's all right to talk," laughed John.

"It's all right to DO, too," asserted Grant positively. "I don't believe there's anything that takes away the best part of a man as surely as gambling. The gambler has no sympathy for any one, his heart is dried up and to my mind he is about the worst specimen you can find anywhere."

At that moment the conversation was interrupted by the firing of the first gun. This was the signal for all the boats to prepare themselves for the coming struggle.

Ross Kay

Several minutes would elapse before the race began and the report was for the warning of the contestants.

The boys now were clad in bathing suits although every one wore a sweater in addition. They were confident that they would speedily be drenched and they were prepared for emergencies. If any accident befell the boat and they were compelled to swim, they would not be hampered by heavy clothing.

It had been agreed that there should not be a flying start. Every boat was to rest on the line and turn on its power after the second signal was given.

As Fred, who was at the wheel glanced along the line of the contestants he counted ten other boats that had entered the race. The only one of the number, however, which he feared was the graceful little motor-boat, only a few yards distant from the place where the Black Growler was resting.

There was no conversation on the boat. The faces of all the Go Ahead boys were tense and drawn and apparently all were unaware of the noise and the presence of the hundreds of interested spectators.

Sam, though he was silent, was not idle. Every minute he was either looking into the machinery or rubbing it with the cloth which he continually held.

"It's time for that gun," said Fred in a low voice.

Every one was watching the face of the little clock on board and as the seconds slowly passed, the boys did not even glance at one another.

In spite of the fact that everything had been done in their power to prepare the Black Growler for the race, the boys were fearful that something had been omitted or overlooked in their preparations.

A silence so tense that it was almost possible to feel it had settled over the region. Even the judges seemed to share in the excitement of the spectators.

The long stillness was broken by the report of the gun.

Instantly every one of the boats on the line started forward.

The Varmint II, and the Black Growler, as we know, were close together and it was speedily evident that the expectations of the assembly were that the former was to be the winner of the race.

"What's the trouble? What's the matter?" demanded George excitedly as the Varmint II was seen to be creeping steadily ahead of its rival.

"Never you mind," said Sam brusquely. "We aren't goin' to be left in this race. If everything keeps up as it ought to and nothin' breaks down, we'll be in ahead at the finish."

The race was far different from that in which the boys had engaged in their track meets. In those contests endurance and a reserve of strength were elements that counted almost as much for success as speed.

In the present race, however, there was no fear of exhaustion and if the Black Growler only held to her course, the Go Ahead boys were satisfied that they had little to fear.

When the Varmint II had gained a lead of about ten feet the distance between the two boats remained stationary. Both now were moving swiftly, the stern of each boat had settled low in the water and the spray from the bow speedily drenched every one on board. All, however, were unmindful of any thought of discomfort. Their eyes occasionally were turned toward their rival, but in the main all were looking straight ahead. The sound of the whistles of the yachts, many of which now were slowly moving in a line parallel to that which the racers were following, apparently indicated the delight of many that the Varmint II was leading. Already it was manifest that the other contesting boats had dropped back, as had been expected. The real race was between the two rivals who now were ahead.

The first lap had been covered and the boats had made the first stake. Here the skill of Sam manifested itself by the sharp turn which he told Fred to make. The lead of ten feet had been decreased by at least a yard. The relative positions of the two boats were maintained while they both sped swiftly toward the next turn.

Taught by their rivals of the advantage a quick turn might bring, the Varmint II here was sharply brought in and a shout of protest arose from the Go Ahead boys when for a moment a collision appeared to be unavoidable. The Black Growler yielded a little in her course, however, and the danger was avoided, although the Varmint II by her trick regained the yard which she had lost at the previous stake.

The boats now were speeding back toward the starting

place. The entire course covered eighteen and three-eighths miles and each boat was supposed to cover the course three times.

When the racing motor-boats drew near the start a chorus of whistles and cries were mingled in the salute which greeted them both.

The sounds to the Go Ahead boys seemed indistinct and far away. They were all intent solely upon what the Varmint II might try to do when the stake was turned.

This time, however, each boat held to its course and the danger of a collision was avoided. Sharply and swiftly both boats made the turn and then, with the Varmint II still leading by nearly ten feet, the second course was begun.

Sam had taken his position directly behind Fred. He seldom spoke to the excited boy, who was handling the wheel with marvelous skill.

"We can turn on more power," suggested Fred.

"We don't want any more now," replied Sam. "Just hold her as she is."

The wind was slightly stronger than it had been a few minutes before and the spray dashed more frequently over the crews of both boats. Somehow the two racing motor-boats had now drawn in so that they were nearer each other by at least two yards than they had been at the start.

When still holding the same relative position the two

swiftly moving boats passed the Caledonia on which Fred's grandfather was the guest of the Stevens', there were several prolonged blasts of the whistle and numerous loud calls from Mr. Button as well as from Miss Susie for the Black Growler to overtake her rival. The sounds, however, were all lost upon the Go Ahead boys whose attention now was centered upon the boat immediately in front of them.

Sam was complacent and apparently confident, but his feelings were not shared by his young friends. To them it seemed as if their efforts to cut down the distance by which the Varmint II was leading were vain. The speed of the two boats apparently was equal. The bows alike flung the water far from either side while the stern of each boat appeared to be almost buried in the midst of the seething, boiling, rushing water.

Far behind them in a long line stretched out the other contestants. There was slight interest in the race now except between the two leading boats, one or the other of which seemed to be certain of the prize.

Apparently the narrow escape from an accident when the turn had been made in the preceding lap had made the crew of each boat more cautious. At all events neither tried to cut in very far upon the other and even on the home stretch in the second lap neither had gained any advantage upon the other.

"It looks as if it was all up," exclaimed George dolefully.

"Never you mind," said Sam. "If we can hold them where they are I think we can do a little better on the home stretch than they can."

"But they may be planning the same thing," protested Fred.

"You just give your attention to your wheel," said Sam. "I guess if you attend to your share, the rest of us will try to look after ours."

On the third and last part of the course even the shrill whistles of the yachts and the cries and cheers that greeted the ears of the Go Ahead boys appeared to take on a sharper edge. The face of every boy was set and drawn. That silver cup in the eyes of all four now appeared to be the most valuable prize that life could offer.

Steadily and swiftly the two boats rounded the first point and then Sam once more began to work. Just what he was doing was not apparent to his companions, but after a few minutes George exclaimed excitedly, "We're gaining on them! We're gaining as sure as you live!"

In a brief time the announcement of the excited boy was manifestly seen to be correct. Slowly and yet steadily the lead of the Varmint II was cut down. Less than six feet now intervened between the two boats.

The supreme moment apparently arrived when the last turn was made. Before them was the home stretch. The last leg of the course was now to be run and here the Black Growler must win if she was to win at all.

As the boat rounded the stake a shout of anger arose from all on board the Black Growler when it was seen that their rival again was trying to cut in upon the course.

"She wants to box us," muttered Sam. "She thinks if she can get right in front of us that we'll have to take her breakers and that we'll not be able to make up any of the distance."

Rising to his feet Sam seized the megaphone and called in his loudest tones, "Don't you try that! We shall ram you if you do. Keep to your own course and we'll keep to ours."

Whether it was Sam's demand or not will never be known, but the course of the Varmint II veered slightly and almost before the boys were aware of the change which had occurred they were side by side with their rival.

As the two boats drew near the finish the excitement on board each apparently was shared by the spectators. The calls and screams and cries redoubled, while the blasts of the whistles were added to the deafening noise. Swiftly and steadily and yet side by side the boats swept forward. To the anxious boys it did not appear that there was any distance between them. Do what they might the Go Ahead boys were unable to increase the speed of their racing motor-boat, which now seemed to be almost below the surface so low was it lying in the water.

The Caledonia meanwhile had moved closer to the line and the excitement on her deck was keener than that on any other boat in the assembly. If Fred's attention had not been so strongly centered upon his task he might have seen his grandfather running back and forth near the rail, his hat in one hand and his cane held midway in the other, shouting in his loudest tones to his grandson to "put on more power and win that race."

Miss Susie already had lost much of her ability to shout. Her voice rose scarcely above a whisper.

Of all these things, however, the Go Ahead boys were ignorant when the two boats swept across the line.

Even those who were on board were not able to say positively which had won the cup.

"That is the worst finish I have ever seen in a race," said Fred to his friends when the Black Growler in a wide semi-circle turned from the course.

"I think it will be for the judges to say anyway," said George as he wrung the water out of his dripping sweater.

"I fancy they will be the ones who will pick the winner," laughed Grant. "I hope they'll not call it a draw and that we shall have to try it all over again."

"I shan't mind very much if they do," said John.

"There's a call from the judges!" interrupted Fred, who had seldom looked away from the judges' boat, which now they were again approaching.

Suddenly a great hush fell over the assembly. Every one anxiously looked toward the boat of the judges, striving to hear the announcement which was about to be made through the megaphone.

"Hold me!" said Fred. "If the Varmint II wins I think I shall need somebody to brace me up."

At that moment, however, the voice of the judge was

heard and when he announced that by a margin of only six inches the Black Growler had won the cup, a shout went up from the crew of the little racing motor-boat that was heard above the din that followed the award.

"That's worth while, Peewee!" declared George as he pounded his diminutive friend upon his back.

"That's what it is!" joined in the other boys.

Meanwhile the victorious motor-boat had drawn alongside the Caledonia and as Fred looked up to the enthusiastic people on the deck the only voice to which he was listening was that of his grandfather.

"That was fine, young man!" shouted the old gentleman. "If you hadn't won that race I think I should have cut you off in my will. I have got a reward here for Sam, too, and you tell him not to leave before he has seen me."

Sam who also had heard the statement made no response until Fred eagerly turned to him and said, "You'll not leave, will you, Sam, without seeing my grandfather?"

Sam smiled as he replied, "Probably not. I don't intend to leave this boat anyway. She won out by six inches in this race but I'm tellin' you this isn't the only race she'll have, and when she is racing I don't intend to be very far away."

Choose from Thousands of 1stWorldLibrary Classics By

A. M. Barnard
Ada Leverson
Adolphus William Ward
Aesop
Agatha Christie
Alexander Aaronsohn
Alexander Kielland
Alexandre Dumas
Alfred Gatty
Alfred Ollivant
Alice Duer Miller
Alice Turner Curtis
Alice Dunbar
Allen Chapman
Alleyne Ireland
Ambrose Bierce
Amelia E. Barr
Amory H. Bradford
Andrew Lang
Andrew McFarland Davis
Andy Adams
Angela Brazil
Anna Alice Chapin
Anna Sewell
Annie Besant
Annie Hamilton Donnell
Annie Payson Call
Annie Roe Carr
Annonaymous
Anton Chekhov
Archibald Lee Fletcher
Arnold Bennett
Arthur C. Benson
Arthur Conan Doyle
Arthur M. Winfield
Arthur Ransome
Arthur Schnitzler
Arthur Train
Atticus
B.H. Baden-Powell
B. M. Bower
B. C. Chatterjee
Baroness Emmuska Orczy
Baroness Orczy
Basil King
Bayard Taylor
Ben Macomber
Bertha Muzzy Bower
Bjornstjerne Bjornson

Booth Tarkington
Boyd Cable
Bram Stoker
C. Collodi
C. E. Orr
C. M. Ingleby
Carolyn Wells
Catherine Parr Traill
Charles A. Eastman
Charles Amory Beach
Charles Dickens
Charles Dudley Warner
Charles Farrar Browne
Charles Ives
Charles Kingsley
Charles Klein
Charles Hanson Towne
Charles Lathrop Pack
Charles Romyn Dake
Charles Whibley
Charles Willing Beale
Charlotte M. Braeme
Charlotte M. Yonge
Charlotte Perkins Stetson
Clair W. Hayes
Clarence Day Jr.
Clarence E. Mulford
Clemence Housman
Confucius
Coningsby Dawson
Cornelis DeWitt Wilcox
Cyril Burleigh
D. H. Lawrence
Daniel Defoe
David Garnett
Dinah Craik
Don Carlos Janes
Donald Keyhoe
Dorothy Kilner
Dougan Clark
Douglas Fairbanks
E. Nesbit
E. P. Roe
E. Phillips Oppenheim
E. S. Brooks
Earl Barnes
Edgar Rice Burroughs
Edith Van Dyne
Edith Wharton

Edward Everett Hale
Edward J. O'Biren
Edward S. Ellis
Edwin L. Arnold
Eleanor Atkins
Eleanor Hallowell Abbott
Eliot Gregory
Elizabeth Gaskell
Elizabeth McCracken
Elizabeth Von Arnim
Ellem Key
Emerson Hough
Emilie F. Carlen
Emily Bronte
Emily Dickinson
Enid Bagnold
Enilor Macartney Lane
Erasmus W. Jones
Ernie Howard Pie
Ethel May Dell
Ethel Turner
Ethel Watts Mumford
Eugene Sue
Eugenie Foa
Eugene Wood
Eustace Hale Ball
Evelyn Everett-green
Everard Cotes
F. H. Cheley
F. J. Cross
F. Marion Crawford
Fannie E. Newberry
Federick Austin Ogg
Ferdinand Ossendowski
Fergus Hume
Florence A. Kilpatrick
Fremont B. Deering
Francis Bacon
Francis Darwin
Frances Hodgson Burnett
Frances Parkinson Keyes
Frank Gee Patchin
Frank Harris
Frank Jewett Mather
Frank L. Packard
Frank V. Webster
Frederic Stewart Isham
Frederick Trevor Hill
Frederick Winslow Taylor

Friedrich Kerst	Hayden Carruth	James Branch Cabell
Friedrich Nietzsche	Helent Hunt Jackson	James DeMille
Fyodor Dostoyevsky	Helen Nicolay	James Joyce
G.A. Henty	Hendrik Conscience	James Lane Allen
G.K. Chesterton	Hendy David Thoreau	James Lane Allen
Gabrielle E. Jackson	Henri Barbusse	James Oliver Curwood
Garrett P. Serviss	Henrik Ibsen	James Oppenheim
Gaston Leroux	Henry Adams	James Otis
George A. Warren	Henry Ford	James R. Driscoll
George Ade	Henry Frost	Jane Abbott
Geroge Bernard Shaw	Henry James	Jane Austen
George Cary Eggleston	Henry Jones Ford	Jane L. Stewart
George Durston	Henry Seton Merriman	Janet Aldridge
George Ebers	Henry W Longfellow	Jens Peter Jacobsen
George Eliot	Herbert A. Giles	Jerome K. Jerome
George Gissing	Herbert Carter	Jessie Graham Flower
George MacDonald	Herbert N. Casson	John Buchan
George Meredith	Herman Hesse	John Burroughs
George Orwell	Hildegard G. Frey	John Cournos
George Sylvester Viereck	Homer	John F. Kennedy
George Tucker	Honore De Balzac	John Gay
George W. Cable	Horace B. Day	John Glasworthy
George Wharton James	Horace Walpole	John Habberton
Gertrude Atherton	Horatio Alger Jr.	John Joy Bell
Gordon Casserly	Howard Pyle	John Kendrick Bangs
Grace E. King	Howard R. Garis	John Milton
Grace Gallatin	Hugh Lofting	John Philip Sousa
Grace Greenwood	Hugh Walpole	John Taintor Foote
Grant Allen	Humphry Ward	Jonas Lauritz Idemil Lie
Guillermo A. Sherwell	Ian Maclaren	Jonathan Swift
Gulielma Zollinger	Inez Haynes Gillmore	Joseph A. Altsheler
Gustav Flaubert	Irving Bacheller	Joseph Carey
H. A. Cody	Isabel Cecilia Williams	Joseph Conrad
H. B. Irving	Isabel Hornibrook	Joseph E. Badger Jr
H.C. Bailey	Israel Abrahams	Joseph Hergesheimer
H. G. Wells	Ivan Turgenev	Joseph Jacobs
H. H. Munro	J.G.Austin	Jules Vernes
H. Irving Hancock	J. Henri Fabre	Julian Hawthrone
H. R. Naylor	J. M. Barrie	Julie A Lippmann
H. Rider Haggard	J. M. Walsh	Justin Huntly McCarthy
H. W. C. Davis	J. Macdonald Oxley	Kakuzo Okakura
Haldeman Julius	J. R. Miller	Karle Wilson Baker
Hall Caine	J. S. Fletcher	Kate Chopin
Hamilton Wright Mabie	J. S. Knowles	Kenneth Grahame
Hans Christian Andersen	J. Storer Clouston	Kenneth McGaffey
Harold Avery	J. W. Duffield	Kate Langley Bosher
Harold McGrath	Jack London	Kate Langley Bosher
Harriet Beecher Stowe	Jacob Abbott	Katherine Cecil Thurston
Harry Castlemon	James Allen	Katherine Stokes
Harry Coghill	James Andrews	L. A. Abbot
Harry Houidini	James Baldwin	L. T. Meade

L. Frank Baum
Latta Griswold
Laura Dent Crane
Laura Lee Hope
Laurence Housman
Lawrence Beasley
Leo Tolstoy
Leonid Andreyev
Lewis Carroll
Lewis Sperry Chafer
Lilian Bell
Lloyd Osbourne
Louis Hughes
Louis Joseph Vance
Louis Tracy
Louisa May Alcott
Lucy Fitch Perkins
Lucy Maud Montgomery
Luther Benson
Lydia Miller Middleton
Lyndon Orr
M. Corvus
M. H. Adams
Margaret E. Sangster
Margret Howth
Margaret Vandercook
Margaret W. Hungerford
Margret Penrose
Maria Edgeworth
Maria Thompson Daviess
Mariano Azuela
Marion Polk Angellotti
Mark Overton
Mark Twain
Mary Austin
Mary Catherine Crowley
Mary Cole
Mary Hastings Bradley
Mary Roberts Rinehart
Mary Rowlandson
M. Wollstonecraft Shelley
Maud Lindsay
Max Beerbohm
Myra Kelly
Nathaniel Hawthrone
Nicolo Machiavelli
O. F. Walton
Oscar Wilde
Owen Johnson
P.G. Wodehouse
Paul and Mabel Thorne

Paul G. Tomlinson
Paul Severing
Percy Brebner
Percy Keese Fitzhugh
Peter B. Kyne
Plato
Quincy Allen
R. Derby Holmes
R. L. Stevenson
R. S. Ball
Rabindranath Tagore
Rahul Alvares
Ralph Bonehill
Ralph Henry Barbour
Ralph Victor
Ralph Waldo Emmerson
Rene Descartes
Ray Cummings
Rex Beach
Rex E. Beach
Richard Harding Davis
Richard Jefferies
Richard Le Gallienne
Robert Barr
Robert Frost
Robert Gordon Anderson
Robert L. Drake
Robert Lansing
Robert Lynd
Robert Michael Ballantyne
Robert W. Chambers
Rosa Nouchette Carey
Rudyard Kipling
Saint Augustine
Samuel B. Allison
Samuel Hopkins Adams
Sarah Bernhardt
Sarah C. Hallowell
Selma Lagerlof
Sherwood Anderson
Sigmund Freud
Standish O'Grady
Stanley Weyman
Stella Benson
Stella M. Francis
Stephen Crane
Stewart Edward White
Stijn Streuvels
Swami Abhedananda
Swami Parmananda
T. S. Ackland

T. S. Arthur
The Princess Der Ling
Thomas A. Janvier
Thomas A Kempis
Thomas Anderton
Thomas Bailey Aldrich
Thomas Bulfinch
Thomas De Quincey
Thomas Dixon
Thomas H. Huxley
Thomas Hardy
Thomas More
Thornton W. Burgess
U. S. Grant
Upton Sinclair
Valentine Williams
Various Authors
Vaughan Kester
Victor Appleton
Victor G. Durham
Victoria Cross
Virginia Woolf
Wadsworth Camp
Walter Camp
Walter Scott
Washington Irving
Wilbur Lawton
Wilkie Collins
Willa Cather
Willard F. Baker
William Dean Howells
William le Queux
W. Makepeace Thackeray
William W. Walter
William Shakespeare
Winston Churchill
Yei Theodora Ozaki
Yogi Ramacharaka
Young E. Allison
Zane Grey

www.ingramcontent.com/pod-product-compliance
Lightning Source LLC
Chambersburg PA
CBHW020605180626
46810CB00007B/2656